Died by Blood, Born by Blood

Died by Blood, Born by Blood

A Vampire Memoir

Kelly Carlson

Published by: Kelly Carlson

ISBN: 979-8-8856713-1-6

Cover: Robyn Mathews-Lingen

Book design: Designwrite Studios

Printed in the United States of America.

First edition.

*To my parents
Gerald and Barbara Carlson*

*and a special thanks to
Patrick Henry
for helping with editing the book*

CONTENTS

PROLOGUE

A long time ago, in a galaxy far, far away … Oops. That opening has already been claimed. But my story will take you to a long time ago—about a millennium—and to somewhere at least far, if not far, far away.

We start in familiar time and territory, though. I'm Solena Wilshire Chilstrom. It's 2021, and we're in New York City. I'm 5'8", have reddish blond hair, and weigh 130 pounds. People say I'm pretty—at least my clients do. I own and manage an escort service called By the Light of the Moon. I cater to the rich. In case you're wondering, yes, it's illegal. But the authorities don't bother me. I have taken care of that.

Here's the unfamiliar territory. I died when I was twenty-eight years old—in the year 991, on the 23rd of July. I lived near the town of York, in a place called Wilshire. My family was wealthy. We were the lords there. I had many friends.

I met the man I still love today, one uneventful evening. What I didn't know is that he would change my life, quite literally forever.

Died By Blood, Born By Blood: A Vampire Memoir

CHAPTER 1

Forever is ... forever

It all started when I was coming home for the evening. I had spent the day in the village with a few friends. I bumped into a young man on the street–at least at the time I thought he was young.

"Excuse me," we said in unison.

I should let you know now. I'm not relating what we said–or rather, how we said it. Had you eavesdropped on this conversation, you'd have thought you were listening to Beowulf instead of Anne Rice. Our language was Old–Very Old–Anglo-Saxon English, and of course it was totally intelligible to us. Twenty-first century American would have been gibberish in our ears. Maybe after my story gets out, some enterprising scholar will take the hint, and come ask me to speak as I did back in the tenth century. Wouldn't it be an academic coup to hear me recite Beowulf!

"You are a very beautiful woman. You are not betrothed already. I do not see a wedding ring on your hand."

This seemed rather abrupt, but I managed a reply. "I choose who I want, not what my family wants. There must be love between us."

"So, you are strong-willed. I like that in women. No spunk, no fun. Please forgive me, I have not told you my name. I'm Edmond Chilstrom."

"Solena Wilshire."

"It has been an honor, Solena. I hope I will see you again."

When I looked back, he was smiling. The rest of the way home I had a weird feeling in my stomach—one I'd never experienced before, but that I liked. I couldn't get him out of my mind.

A couple of weeks later I was riding my favorite horse, Misty, in the woods in the evening. I saw Edmond in the moonlight. He looked different this time, really pale. It's hard to explain.

His face was ghostly white. But it was more. A crazed, hungry look in his eyes. It looked like he was hunting. But humans don't hunt that way.

He turned around, saw me—and disappeared. You'll find it odd, but I shrugged it off and didn't think about it.

Another fortnight passed. My parents and I were having a party for some friends, and I saw him again. Edmond was invited to the party, though I hadn't known this.

"Solena, how nice to see you again! I must apologize for not being a gentleman the last time I saw you. I had not eaten yet, and was quite hungry. I had no fresh meat at home, and was short of money."

"No need to apologize, Edmond. Everybody's been hungry one time or another."

"I'd be delighted if you'd take a walk with me in the woods. The moon is full, the stars are shining."

As we were looking at the moon, he moved closer to me. His arm was around the small of my back. My back arched. I pulled my eyes toward his. I kissed him long and deep. It seemed to last forever, but not long enough. I felt truly loved for the first time in my life.

We made passionate love for hours as the moon shone on us in the gentle surroundings of the forest. All night Edmond seemed to be getting stronger. Eventually he pressed his lips on my neck, but it didn't feel like a kiss. I felt sharp pricks. At that moment he pulled away and left, saying he loved me.

With my voice and body I responded, "I will love you forever, too!"

I just lay there for a while. When I came out of my daze, I went home. My parents were understandably worried, but I assured them I was all right.

As months went by, Edmond and I saw more and more of each other. I really loved him. But something was peculiar. I saw him only at night.

On our three-month anniversary he took me to the same spot in the woods as on that first evening. He brought delicious food and fine wine, but didn't eat or drink any of it. I thought this strange, but I was too much in love to be concerned.

Edmond sat me down on a rock and went to his knees. He reached into his pocket. He put an emerald ring, with a solid gold band and diamonds, on my finger. "Solena, you are my one and truest love. This love is never dying. I want you to be with me forever."

"Yes?"

"Would you do me the honor to be my wife?"

"To marry you would be the most wonderful thing in the world! I don't know what I'd have done if you hadn't asked me. Of course I will marry you!"

He picked me up and swung me around. "You have no idea what you mean to me."

It was almost dawn when we got up to leave. "Please come home with me to tell my parents. We should both be there."

"I wish I could, but I can't. I must go home myself. I will see you this evening. I love you."

He ran off in a hurry. I stayed and watched the sunrise. I miss the sunrise the most. ... But I'm getting ahead of the story.

When I told my parents, they were so happy for me. "Why isn't Edmond with you?" I didn't really understand myself.

About an hour after sunset, Edmond arrived at Wilshire Manor. He already knew my parents–he had come to their party.

He was very neatly dressed–white cotton shirt, loose fitting pants, long leather boots. He is six feet tall, and looked taller. He wore a wool cloak to keep warm. He bowed to my parents and kissed my hand.

"I am pleased to see you again, Lord and Lady Wilshire. Be assured that your daughter will be safe with me, forever."

The next week we were married at Wilshire Manor, and I became Solena Chilstrom.

The ceremony was beautiful–lit torches, proper dress. Around midnight we left for our home. When we arrived, Edmond said he needed to tell me something. He was afraid that on hearing it, I would leave him. I thought he was going to tell me he had been married before, but it certainly wasn't that.

"Solena, I am five hundred years old. Don't say anything yet. I know you can't believe this. I didn't believe it five hundred years ago. I was thirty years old. I know what you're thinking; I didn't believe it either."

"Edmond, how is it possible? Nobody can be five hundred years old!"

"Solena, I was alive, or dead already, when Christianity was brought to England by St. Augustine. I lived in the south. My family had died away, and people in my village were very suspicious; they would have killed me. So I moved north, taking my family's wealth with me, and moved from village to village. Finally I settled here, near York. I have occupied many empty cottages and added to them, so I could live there by day. I have also slept in the ground.

"If I live in a village, I have to move every five or ten years. If I live in the woods, I can stay there longer, for hundreds of years if I have to. I enjoy living. Humans can be dangerous. But you are not."

"Edmond, what do you mean, humans are dangerous? You are human, right?"

"I was once human, but not anymore. My human life ended five hundred years ago. I was robbed and stabbed in the woods. A man found me. He saw I was dying. He was a vampire, so he could save me. But to save me he had to kill me. So I became a vampire."

"A vampire? I've heard legends about them, but you don't match the stories. I've never really believed in them. When a person dies, they die. They can't come back."

"But I did come back."

"Edmond, please tell me the truth."

"I am. This vampire never told me his name. He didn't have to change me. I don't know why he chose to. He just decided to make me immortal. He put me in a dark place for the day. He came back the next couple of nights and showed me what to do. I never saw him again. You must have questions. Haven't you wondered why I don't eat or drink? Or why you see me only after dark?"

"Yes, I have wondered. I thought you didn't like sunlight, but the not eating and no drinking confused me. Maybe you liked to eat in private. I just can't believe it. It seems so unreal."

"Aren't you scared of me, Solena?"

"No, I'm not. I know I can trust you. Otherwise, I wouldn't have married you. I know you love me and I you. Drinking blood frightens me, but you have never scared me. What else can you do? Can you turn into a bat?"

"No, I can't turn into a bat, but I can fly. As you've seen, I can run very fast. Swords and knives can't hurt me, but a stake through the heart can. So can fire and sunlight. But water can't; I've never understood why not, or why we can't go near crosses and holy water burns us. Decapitation will also kill us, like everybody else.

"There are advantages and disadvantages to being a vampire– as there are with everything. Now I'm going to give you my wedding gift, if you still want to be with me."

"Edmond, I love you. Why would I leave you?"

"Because, if you don't accept my wedding gift, I will leave you."

"What are you talking about?"

"My wedding gift is immortality. I don't want to see you grow old and die. I've seen my family die, and I don't like it. Do you accept my gift? I don't offer it to just anybody."

"If it's the only way I can be with you, then I accept. I would die if I couldn't be with you. So, what do we do now?"

CHAPTER 2

It's hard to do the first time

That night we made love–the last time I would do this as a human. I'll tell you this: it's better when you're immortal. You have keener senses.

In the morning I watched the sunrise. I'll never forget it. I also watched the sunset in the evening. By the way, vampires wake when the sun is gone, but it is okay to see the colored sky right after the sun has gone down.

I spent that day with my family and friends. I ate rich foods and drank sweet wines. I would never be able to enjoy these pleasures again. I still remember what they taste like, but the memory is fading.

I miss being human. Vampires have special powers, but not as many freedoms as humans. During the day we must find shelter or we die.

I'm getting off track again; please excuse me.

Before I left Wilshire Manor for the last time as a human, I took several jewels that would have passed down to me from my parents anyway (I was an only child). The jewels have sustained me through the years, during the tough times.

When I got back home, Edmond was up and bathing. I was shocked. "Edmond, I thought vampires don't like water!"

"Water does not harm vampires. As I've said, that is an ugly rumor, like so many others, such as that we can't cross running water. I guess I forgot to tell you a few things. Now I've got to tell you what we discover when we first drink blood from a victim—which you'll do tomorrow night."

"Why not tonight, Edmond?"

"You must die and sleep first. You have to build up a thirst before you can drink from a victim. Come with me into the bedroom. I have already fed. I have enough blood to transform you and keep my strength at the same time."

That night we made plans; they'll be revealed later. At around three in the morning, Edmond sat down on the bed.

"Solena, you can still change your mind. If you go through with this, you will never be the same. You remember the night we became engaged, I said, 'You have no idea what you mean to me'? Well, now you're finding out. Children will be out of the question, and everything else human. Do you realize all this?"

"Yes, I do. I've thought about it. But being with you is more important than what I'm giving up."

Edmond started kissing me. We moved closer to the bed and lay down. Slowly, he moved down my neck while still kissing me. Suddenly I felt something sharp on my neck. It was an abrupt stab of pain. Then, as he was drinking, something strange happened.

My mind wandered away. I saw myself growing up in northern England, at Wilshire Manor. I saw my first meeting with Edmond, then the second—how weird it was and how odd he acted. Then I saw my funeral. "I'm not dead yet," I thought. My parents were mourning my death. Then I saw their deaths. My aunt and uncle moved into Wilshire Manor. I saw their children growing up and continuing the family.

Edmond withdrew his teeth. He opened his shirt, took a knife, and made a cut in his chest. I saw his blood, wanted it, but was too weak to reach for it. He moved closer to me, and a drop of blood oozed into my mouth. It tasted sweet and salty. I wanted more.

I grabbed Edmond with all the strength I had left and pulled him down. I was like a hungry beast that hadn't eaten for days. I don't remember how long I drank, but I do remember how good it felt.

"Sleep now, my love. You must sleep for the change to be complete."

When I awoke, I felt like I could fly.

"Of course you can fly, my darling. You are now a vampire."

"Edmond, you can read my mind?"

"That was a surprise I saved for you. You can too. But now you must get up. Come, look at yourself in the mirror."

I was shocked when I saw myself–beauty that was never there before. But there was also a sign that life was dead.

"Now, Solena, welcome to the land of the undead."

I looked around the room. It was made of stone. The door kept light out, but I could see better than any human could. I was standing by a stone coffin. It was cushioned inside.

"I hate sleeping in hard places. Don't you, Solena?"

This room had no way for air to enter. I realized I was not breathing anymore.

"Don't be alarmed. Your body doesn't need to breathe. Any air in the room is sucked out when the door is opened, and this means humans, who might want to hurt us, can't enter. Let's get out of this discouraging room. Coffins depress me. I have a surprise for you."

"What is it?"

Then I knew what it was. I could smell blood. It was not from Edmond's supper.

"You must be hungry. I know I am when I wake up in the evening. This must sound strange to you–'waking in the evening'?"

"Not anymore, since I don't have a choice."

We walked into another room. A young boy, frightened and confused, cowered in the corner. I could smell his blood. My thirst was rising.

"Will his family miss him? I wouldn't want them to worry."

"He won't be missed. He's an orphan. You will be doing him a favor by sending him to his parents. He wishes they were with him right now. I found him wandering through the streets a couple of nights ago, I gave him food and water. I read in his mind that his parents died."

I was hungry. I walked towards him. He ran, but I was too fast. I grabbed him gently. "Don't worry, little boy."

I didn't want to know his name. If I had, I couldn't have killed him.

"You will be with your parents soon. I'm certain they miss you. My parents miss me, I miss them, and I'm sure you miss yours. Don't you want to be with them?"

"Well, I do, lady, but I don't want to die."

"It is the only way you can be with them."

I picked him up and brought his neck towards my sharp canine teeth (they really surprised me). I bit into his neck and tasted the sweet, life-giving nectar. I could feel his life draining away and mine growing stronger. The moment his life ended, my canines retracted.

"Very good, my love. The change is complete–you are now truly dead. This is the only time you have to kill. You only have to end one life–except for certain ceremonies. Otherwise, you know when you have to stop.

"Vampires don't kill. We make the victim lose all will power. The victim will forget what happened. But sometimes we have to kill–as I said, some ceremonies require it, and sometimes we have to defend ourselves. Just like humans."

After I fed we went outside, so I could discover the world of the vampire.

"I have to warn you, as I've already said. Stay away from holy water and crosses. They will burn our skin. I don't know why. I don't fear God, but maybe it's because God is pure and good, and we are considered evil. We are unwanted in this world. People hunt us down and kill us. Now, would you like to learn how to fly?"

"Of course!"

"This is something all vampires should know. This is how we travel long distances. And it's fun! Solena, jump up in the air as high as you can, but think of flying. If you don't think of it, you won't. When you want to land, just land."

I did what Edmond said. You feel so free. I saw sights I'd never seen before. My house looked so small. Landing was easy. I tested other powers. My speed was even faster than when I chased the boy; it was like I disappeared. I lifted heavy boulders. I could control another person's mind.

Around three in the morning we returned to the airless room. "Why isn't there any dirt in the coffin?" I asked.

"We don't have to sleep on our home soil. As I said, a lot of the so-called information about vampires is false. Since our home soil isn't required, it's easier to travel."

I never thought I would climb into a coffin while I was awake and alert. As the sun rose, my eyes immediately closed. I didn't even dream. I slept like the dead. This makes sense—I am dead.

When night came, I was awakened by my husband. "Come, my love. I'm hungry, and I suspect you are too. I'll show you the proper way to hunt for the rest of your life."

We went into the woods. Along came two woodsmen.

"Excuse me, could you tell us if we're near a village?" Edmond asked. "We're hungry, and would like to eat."

"A couple of miles from here. We can show you the way. We're going there ourselves."

"Is there any way we can repay you?"

"Not necessary. Our chance to do a good deed is payment in full."

Edmond looked at the woodsmen. "You will not remember meeting us. This is just an ordinary night for you. You will be tired. You'll think you didn't get enough sleep."

Edmond easily caught one of the men, I the other. Edmond moved him so his neck was showing. I could see the blood flowing in his veins. When Edmond was finished, the man walked away in a daze. The wound in his neck was already healing.

"Now, Solena, it's your turn. Look at him, look into his eyes. Tell him to forget what happened and what is going to happen. It is easy."

I wasn't sure I could do it, but "Here goes."

There was terror in his eyes. My thirst thrived on that terror. "You will not remember anything about this meeting."

The man's face went blank. He had no self-control. My sharp teeth came out. I bit into his sweet-smelling neck. The blood flowed into my mouth.

I began to fill up with a warm glow. My teeth withdrew when I was full. The man walked away in a stupor.

Edmond looked at me as if I had achieved something. "Very good, my love. It's hard to do the first time. You make a much better vampire than most of the others I've met. By the way, you'll meet more vampires; we're drawn to each other. I stay away from them, though; some like to kill every night."

"I thought we couldn't do that."

"We can, but only if we force our teeth back out. It's difficult to do when full. I won't do that. I hate to end human life."

"What else can you tell me about what we can do?"

"You will be able to sense the vampires you make. You have exchanged blood with them. You will be connected forever. You will know when their life ends, they will know when you die."

"So, you and I will always be connected. That's nice to know!"

"Come, Solena. We have to plan our mortal deaths."

"I will miss my family. My parents are dear to me."

"So were mine to me. I had no help with this part when I died. So, you are lucky."

"What do you have in mind? The plans we made earlier?"

"In about a week we will be robbed. The robber will kill us and burn the house down."

"How will he burn our daytime quarters?"

"I can switch the systems. I don't always burn my residences down. Most of the time I save them. Are you prepared to never see your parents again?"

"I'd not have become a vampire if I wasn't prepared for that."

"Sometimes losing the family will sway people away from vampirism. I'm glad it didn't change your mind."

"Edmond, my love for you is greater than my love for my parents. That sounds cruel, but I like this kind of love more."

The sun was about to rise, so we went home, and made love. Then we went to bed. I still miss my parents, and I always will. But I have had a good long life. My powers make life interesting and fun.

CHAPTER 3

Something was missing

That night my parents joined us for the evening.

"Welcome to our home. We're honored to have you here." I had fixed some food, but Edmond and I ate nothing.

"What a lovely house this is. Edmond, how long have you lived here?"

"About ten years. I should have invited you here before. How rude of me not to!"

"Well, we're happy to finally see where you and our daughter live," my mother said.

"Why aren't you eating with us?" my father asked.

"I have taken up Edmond's habit of eating in private. When you're in love, you change to get along better with the other person."

"Solena, have you seen your jewels?"

"Yes, Mother, I have them. Remember, you wanted me to wear them to the party you are having. By the way, Edmond and I will have to be late. I can't show up without the jewels, so I picked them up the last time I was at Wilshire Manor."

Suddenly there was a noise outside. Edmond ran to see what it was. He yelled at somebody.

"Who was it?"

"I couldn't see, Solena. Maybe your parents should go home. It may not be safe here any longer tonight."

"Edmond is right, Solena. Lady Wilshire, should we take the jewels home with us?"

"No, Father. I mean, please don't. It isn't proper for me to enter the party without them on."

"They may not be safe. Solena, we don't want them stolen."

"We have a place to put them where they won't be found."

"Solena, dear, they should be going now. We can walk them home."

The moon was full. As we were walking back to our house, we saw a man. He came up to Edmond and asked if he had done a good job. Edmond nodded. The man walked away.

"What was that about?"

"Solena, tonight we are going to die in the eyes of the mortal world. I set that up. I wanted your parents to suspect something. It makes it easier to believe."

"What do you mean?"

"We are going to be robbed and killed tonight. The house will be burnt down. I have already packed. Be ready to leave. We have many miles to travel tonight, and we are running out of darkness."

"I am ready to leave my mortal life, for good–even though I know I have already left it."

We each had a bag. I carried my jewels. Edmond said I wouldn't need to take many clothes; he knew someone who would make them for us.

Edmond started a fire in the living room. At that moment I watched my mortal life die right before my eyes, and my immortal life with Edmond begin. We walked out of our burning house, happy, very happy.

We jumped up in the air and flew away. We hovered for a little to watch the people gather. My mother was crying while my father tried to comfort her. I could read their thoughts–"We will miss her so much!" I felt very sad at the moment, and very happy. I was with the man I loved–and would be with him forever.

We started moving again. Flying faster and faster. About an hour later I saw a castle.

"We are here, Solena. Let me show you our new home. Ever since I met you, I've wanted to take you here and live here with you."

We landed. I walked up to the castle. It was even more lovely on the ground than from the sky.

There was a bed in the middle of the main room. We made love. "What a wonderful way to bless this house!" I thought. Then we slept through the day.

We awoke right after sunset. "Good evening, Solena. Are you ready to feed? There is plenty to eat here."

We walked outside, stars shining, moon full. After we had fed, it started to cloud up. By the time we got home it was pouring. It sounded even louder than when I was a mortal. I felt so different. Tonight everything was resolved. My life was complete.

For two hundred years I was happy. But, increasingly, I felt something was missing. I wanted children. Edmond had told me it was out of the question, but I missed having someone to take care of. I didn't have to take care of Edmond, or he of me.

Meanwhile, in a town miles away, a family was being destroyed by lies.

To understand the family dynamic, you have to understand the parents. The family was very poor. The parents considered the children a burden. They used them for labor more than anything else. By day the children would beg for food. Of what the children brought home, the parents gave them little, if any.

It's no surprise that the children resented their parents. Annabelle and Josephine were very protective of their younger brother. He was the one who got the brunt of the parents' frustration. When a neighbor approached the family accusing the children of stealing, the parents didn't believe their denials.

"Annabelle, how could you and your sister and brother steal, especially from our neighbor?"

"But, Father, we didn't. His son did, and said we did. We saw him!"

The father was not buying it. "Mother, do you believe what they did? They have disgraced our family."

The parents had never believed their children–Annabelle, who was sixteen, Josephine, fifteen, and Arthur, fourteen.

"I can't stand to look at their faces anymore," said their mother. "You children are banished from this home. I never want to see you in this village again. We have no children now. Our children are dead."

"But Mother," cried Josephine, "Annabelle is telling the truth. The boy lied. We did not steal from his father."

"Please believe us," Arthur pleaded.

"Arthur, get out of this house with your sisters. I agree with your mother. You are no longer our children."

The children grabbed their belongings and walked out. At the door, they turned to look at their parents one last time. There was no sadness in the parents' eyes. In a final gesture, without any feeling, their mother gave them some food to take.

It seemed like they had walked for days, though they had barely started, when they walked by the boy they had seen commit the theft. That encounter would be seared in their memory.

After a week they were running out of food. Arthur, exhausted, fell to the ground. His sisters picked him up and continued on their journey.

Edmond and I, after feeding, went walking in the woods. We saw two girls carrying a boy. One girl had long strawberry-blond hair, was about 5'2" tall, and wore a ragged dress. The other girl was taller, had long blond hair, and also a ragged dress. The boy was younger. He also had blond hair, shoulder-length and tied back.

"Please help us!" said the first girl. "My name is Annabelle, and this is my sister Josephine. Our brother Arthur is ill."

"Where are your parents?" asked Edmond.

"They don't want us anymore."

"What do you mean, they don't want you?" I probed in astonishment.

"We were accused of stealing, but we didn't do it," Josephine replied.

Arthur had started to stir. We brought the children to the castle, Edmond carrying Arthur, who lost consciousness again.

While I went to get them some food, Edmond said, "Come let me show you to our spare bedrooms. You two must sleep while my wife, Solena, and I will take care of your brother. My name is Edmond Chilstrom. You are our honored guests."

"Thank you, kind sir," said Annabelle.

"Edmond, I insist. And my wife goes by Solena."

"This is very kind of you, Edmond. We will only stay the night. We have no choice but to go to the next village."

"We will see, Annabelle. We will see. It is a long trip to the next village. You are welcome to stay here awhile."

"We don't want to be any bother," said Josephine.

"Oh, it is no bother," I said as I entered the room. "You are welcome here as long as you need. I should go tend to Arthur; we need to get food and water into him."

"No, let me do it. He is mine and Josephine's brother."

"Don't be ridiculous. You two must eat and then rest. You've had a long journey."

They sat down and ate while I went upstairs to take care of Arthur. I still knew how to tend to mortals.

After the girls were asleep, I went downstairs to join Edmond.

"Do you remember when we were talking about what we missed about being human?" I asked. "There are three kids upstairs with no one to take care of them. I would like to."

"That is not possible. We are not mortal."

"It can be done. This is the one thing I really miss, having children."

"People would miss them."

"No one would. Their parents disowned them. It's clear they have no other family. I think we should take care of them."

"They'd think we are strange. Solena. We can't take that chance with our lives."

"Edmond, we're not taking chances. They are young. Young people have more open minds. Come look at them, asleep. They are like little angels."

"You are right, my dear. They are sleeping angels. That is what scares me. Angels can turn into devils overnight. But you're right again, life isn't worth living if you don't take chances. We can talk to them tomorrow night."

Annabelle was obviously the one in charge, so Edmond left a hypnotic suggestion in her mind. We knew her sister and brother would listen to her.

The next night, when we came out of our bedroom, they were still there, eating the food we had left them. Arthur was up, and feeling better.

"We were waiting to say goodbye. We must thank you for your hospitality. But we have been too much of a burden on you already."

"Annabelle, you and your siblings are no burden at all. In fact, we would like you to stay with us. You have no family."

"We have each other," answered Josephine.

"That is true," said Edmond. "But we would like you to join our family. We cannot have children, but it has always been our dream to be a real family."

"You have done so much for us already. Taking us in would be too much," said Arthur, his mouth full of food.

"Arthur, don't be rude!" yelled Annabelle. "We are their guests. You know how to act in someone else's house!"

"Apologize, Arthur!" added Josephine.

"I'm sorry for talking with my mouth full. I am just so hungry."

"That is all right. We understand. Edmond and I are serious about this offer. You need a place to live, and we want someone to take care of."

"Dear hosts, we would love to stay here. I knew you were nice people from the very beginning!" said Annabelle.

I had to snicker. We are not people anymore, we are vampires.

"So you will stay? Please tell us, we want to know," Edmond responded.

"Yes, we will stay," answered Josephine. "There was no doubt, when you asked us. This is more hope than we have felt in a week. When our parents kicked us out, we were devastated."

"We must tell you something about us. You can change your mind after you hear this. But if you do change your mind, you will forget what we are about to say."

"Yes, Edmond, we sort of understand."

"Solena and I are vampires–but we won't hurt you. This is the reason we can't have children."

"Vampires! I know what they are," said Josephine. "Vampires don't scare me."

Arthur and Annabelle had the strangest look on their faces, while Josephine had a look of wonder. We could tell they weren't scared. They knew they were safe with us, and we knew we were safe with them. They didn't ask many questions.

Josephine filled them in. She was correct in almost every respect. She said she had met a vampire once before. He did not hurt her either. This is why she knew we were safe.

It had taken two hundred years, but we had started a family.

CHAPTER 4

That's the way it works

The children accepted our habits quite fast. We made sure they had food on the table every night. They even started sleeping during the day.

We hired a servant to help with the children. Dahlia was an older woman who had no children and had recently lost her husband. She treated our children like they were her own.

They were interested to hear what the country was like 200 years ago and 700 years ago. They marveled that we could fly. Sometimes we took them hunting with us, but we never told them where we slept.

Nine years passed. Annabelle, Josephine, and Arthur had grown up to be beautiful adults.

Edmond and I thought they would leave soon, but we wanted them to be with us forever. We hoped they would make the choice I had.

"My dear children," said Edmond, "you have reached the point in your life when you should get married and earn a living."

"Or there is another option," I added.

"What is the alternative, Mother?" asked Josephine, now twenty-four and looking a lot like me. Annabelle was shorter, but beautiful too, and Arthur was extraordinarily handsome. Whenever he went into town, girls adored him. "Girls want to marry me all the time!" They all loved the area, and didn't want to leave.

"The other option," answered Edmond, "is that you can become one of us, just like your mother chose over 200 years ago."

"We can become vampires?" said Annabelle. "I thought you didn't offer immortality to other people."

"Only to people we really love and don't want to see leave," I responded.

"But Mother, all children leave sometime."

"I know that, Arthur, but we don't want it to happen soon. If you don't want to be what we are, you will not remember us. This is for our safety. Some people want to kill us. Vampire hunters might be able to get information from you."

"But we wouldn't tell!" said Josephine. "We love you both and would never do anything to hurt you."

"Before you make up your mind," I cautioned, "we want to know the whole story about you and your parents. You will understand later."

Annabelle started telling what happened.

"We lived by a shopkeeper and his spoiled son, who could never get enough from his father. His mother had died of consumption when he was a baby. We got along with him, though we weren't friends.

"He would steal from his father, hoping he wouldn't notice. But one day he did. 'Where did the merchandise go?' 'The kids down the street took it.' He actually planted a few items in our cottage.

"The shopkeeper came to see our parents and told them what his son had told him.

"Our parents confronted us. We told them we didn't do it, that we had been set up.

"They didn't believe us. They kicked us out. The boy just laughed as we walked away.

"You have taught us skills and loved us. This is more than we ever got from our parents. I know what I want to do. I can't speak for Josephine or Arthur, but I don't want to leave you."

"That goes for me, too," said Josephine.

"And me," Arthur chimed in.

"Do you know what you will miss out on?" I asked.

"We already know, by living the way you live."

"That makes sense, Arthur, but you can never be mortal again, or have children."

"But you two have children," retorted Annabelle. "You have us. And as Josephine and I can attest, not all women feel the need to have children. We have learned from you that people can choose different styles of life."

"Arthur, what about you?" I asked.

"It has been obvious that your life has intrigued me. I love the smell of the hunt. And what a thrill to hunt but not kill humans. So, I want to be a vampire, just like I said."

"So, you three are sure?" I said, and then I started to walk out.

"Mother, where are you going?"

"Annabelle, I will be gone for a while. It may be a day, I don't know. You will not be transformed until I get home. Watch the sunrise, eat rich foods, stay up all day, sleep at night–so you'll remember what it's like."

I stepped out the door, fed, and flew away. I read their minds, so I knew where their village was, and the names of their parents and the boy who framed them.

When I arrived at the village it was nearing sunrise, so I found a place to sleep for the day. The next night I asked around the village. I learned that the boy, Charles, had been caught stealing, and the shock of the crime killed his father, the shopkeeper. The parents had been shunned, along with the boy, for what they had done.

I found out where the parents were by signaling in on their thoughts. I told them their kids were safe. They didn't care. Charles didn't either.

I insisted they travel to our house. I got them horses to speed up their journey. Then I flew home, arriving close to sunrise.

"How did it go?" asked Edmond.

"Just fine. They'll be arriving in a couple of days."

Annabelle, Josephine, and Arthur were waking up.

"Enjoy these last days of mortal life. It is time for Edmond and me to go to bed. You will find out the purpose of my trip later."

Two days later the parents and Charles arrived. (The children were gone that day.) Dahlia led them into a special room and locked the door.

"They are in the cell, waiting for you."

"Thank you. I trust you fed them and gave them water. Where are the children? Did they see the victims enter the house?"

"No, madam. They were in town."

"Make sure they have food for one more day. The transformation cannot take place tonight. They must sleep first. Where are the children?"

"They are waiting for you in the drawing room. I told them what you told me to say. They are very curious about what is going to happen tonight."

"Very good, Dahlia. Come back tomorrow, but leave before the sun sets. You won't want to be here tomorrow night. You will also remember nothing of what you have done here today; it will seem to have been just a normal day. Tomorrow, feed them once more, then take their belongings away from them, except their clothes. They will let you. Remember: Be out of here before sunset!"

She left for the night. Edmond and I went out to feed. When we returned, the children were still in the drawing room.

"Mother, Father, where have you been?"

"We were out feeding, Arthur. Are you three ready for your transformation to the undead?"

"We are ready, Mother."

I took Arthur, Edmond took Josephine.

Arthur sat down on his bed, and I sat next to him. "This won't hurt much. There is only a sharp prick of pain. Are you ready?"

My teeth came out. Arthur stared at them. I let him touch them. He even punctured his finger on them. I hugged his chest. I gently pushed his head down, and his white neck was staring at me. I could see the blood pulsing. My teeth broke through his skin. He gasped. The hot blood flowed into my mouth.

Slowly, Arthur's body got weaker. When I pulled out, his body dropped on the bed. I took a knife and cut my chest open. Arthur saw the blood and opened his mouth. Some blood dropped in. He swallowed it. He grabbed me with all the strength he had left and pulled me down. When his mouth touched my neck, I could feel him pulling the blood out of me.

I hadn't felt this for 200 years. I didn't see what I had seen when I died. I saw blackness. I was getting weaker. I had enough strength, though, because I had fed earlier. When I attempted to pull away, Arthur tried to stop me.

"You have had enough. You should sleep now, my son. You will wake next night fully dead."

Arthur fell asleep. I carried him to where we sleep. Edmond had added three coffins. Arthur and Josephine looked dead already, though they were still dying.

We went to where Annabelle was. She was sitting on her bed.

"Annabelle, what's wrong?" I asked.

"I'm scared, Mother."

"There's no need to be frightened. You should join your sister and brother soon."

"I would like to take a walk first, if you two don't mind. I'd actually like for you to join me."

"We would love to. You may choose who you want to transform you. Your mother and I just want you to be happy."

We walked for several hours. Annabelle asked us questions, and we answered as honestly as we could. It was about two hours to sunrise when we returned home.

"Father, I would like you to change me."

"I would be honored, as I was when I changed your mother and sister."

I watched them walk into her bedroom. I was never invited to watch this, and I didn't expect to be.

Edmond brought her out, carried her down the stairs to the crypt, and placed her in the last coffin. Then we closed the lids on all three of them. We had our children, finally—our vampire children.

When we awoke, they were still asleep, so we went upstairs to prepare the victims. They were placed in the children's rooms, according to which one the child wanted revenge on the most—the mother in Josephine's room, Charles in Annabelle's, and the father in Arthur's. We also had three other victims in reserve, in case the children didn't want to kill their tormentors. But we were quite sure they didn't care for them anymore. This was our gift to them.

We heard rustling. "Mother, Father, who are the people in the cells downstairs? It's part of the castle we've never seen before."

"No need to worry about them," said Edmond. "How do you three feel?"

"Strange," answered Josephine. "I feel alive, but a part of me has died."

"It hasn't died yet, but it is about to. Your bodies are still in the process of dying. For the course to be complete, you must drink," I said.

"What do you mean, Mother?" asked Annabelle.

"You must kill your first victim, then you don't have to kill anymore. If you don't kill the first victim, your body will die from starvation."

"Father, we really have to kill a person?"

"Yes, Annabelle, that's the way it works."

"Come upstairs with me, Annabelle," I said. "We have a surprise for you."

When we reached her bedroom, and Edmond joined us, I said, "This is our gift to you. You don't have to take him; we have other people downstairs in the cells. This one was chosen for you because you hated him the most.

"I know you are hungry; I can see it in your eyes. I have seen that look in Edmond's eyes before. And I have seen it in the three of you tonight. So, you must do this. If you decide not to feed on Charles, Edmond or I will. But in that case he won't die. This is your chance to get even with him, and this is the only chance you will ever have."

"Oh, Mother, I would love to take him!"

Edmond intervened. "I must do something first."

Edmond walked toward Charles and instructed him to come out of his trance.

"Where am I?"

"You are in a castle in the woods."

"What am I doing here?"

"You are a gift to our daughter, as a gift from her parents."

"What do you mean, a gift to your daughter?"

At that point, Annabelle walked into the room. Charles's face went blank. Edmond left the room and closed the door.

"Charles, you ruined our life with our parents."

"Your life was ruined already. You never got along with your parents."

"Our relationship was bad, but at least tolerable, until you set us up. That is when it crumbled. We cannot forgive our parents and you. Now I am going to pay you back."

The thirst was rising in her. She felt her canine teeth coming out. She could smell the blood in him. He ran from her, but was backed into a wall. Annabelle came up to him and pushed his head to the side. She bit into his neck. She tasted the sweet blood, but it was different from the night before.

She drank and drank. Her strength was growing. She could feel Charles getting weaker. When he was dead, her teeth retracted. He dropped to the floor.

Annabelle went to the mirror and saw herself for the first time. She wasn't pale. Her skin was pinker than usual. She felt like she wasn't alive, but more alive than she had ever felt before.

We were waiting downstairs for Annabelle. "How do you feel?" I asked.

"I have never felt this way before. What does this feeling mean?"

"It means you have finished dying. You are now truly undead. Please sit down. Let your sister take her turn now."

We took Josephine upstairs to her bedroom. "What is my mother doing here?"

"This is our gift to you. You may take her, or we have others downstairs. You may have seen them already. It is your choice. We know you hated your mother even more than your sister and brother did, but you don't have to kill her."

"Mother, I want to kill her! She was awful to us. So was our father. I have no problem with my mother as my first victim. When we were walking in the woods we decided we could never forgive. Do you think I am being unfair?"

"No. I asked your parents, when I found them, if they were sorry for what they had done. They said they weren't. If you are ready, I will prepare her for you."

"Yes, Mother, I am ready. And I am very hungry."

I took the mother out of her trance. She also asked where she was, and I told her. But unlike Edmond, I didn't tell her why she was here.

Josephine walked into the room, and her mother tried to hug her.

"Josephine, where have you been? Your father and I have been so worried about you three."

"No, you have not, Mother. That won't work with me. My mother told me what you said when she asked if you were sorry. I can't forgive you. We can't."

"People can make mistakes, Josephine. And what do you mean, 'your mother told you what I said'? I'm your mother–you can have only one!"

"Not anymore. I have one now who loves me."

Her sister and brother came into the bedroom.

"Do you two not forgive me also?"

Arthur and Annabelle were startled to see their mother, but not surprised.

"We cannot forgive you either."

"I don't believe you three are saying this!"

Along with Annabelle and Arthur, I walked out of the room. It was clear they felt no remorse.

Josephine closed the door.

"Josephine, what are you doing?"

"I have to drink someone's blood until death, then I will die–and become immortal."

"You mean that woman is a vampire?"

"Yes, and so is Annabelle. I will be one soon, and Arthur when he's done with your husband, whom I refuse to call our father."

"You are going to drink my blood?"

She was so stricken with fear that she couldn't move.

Josephine did to her as Annabelle had done to Charles. Afterwards, like her sister, she looked in the mirror. She came downstairs smiling. She felt powerful, like no one could stop her.

"Does this feeling last?" she asked.

"Yes, it does," Edmond replied. "You will never again feel human—because you are not human anymore. Arthur, are you ready?"

"Yes, Father."

"Come with me. Your gift is waiting for you." I stayed behind. This was to be between fathers and son.

Arthur opened his bedroom door and was not surprised. "Father, I want him. I accept my gift."

Edmond brought the father out of a trance, then left. It was just Arthur and his father.

"Son, where have you been?"

"That won't work with me. I no longer care for you."

Josephine and Annabelle glanced into the room, and nodded goodbye to their father. He ran toward them, but Arthur stopped him. "You are going nowhere. You are only going to die."

Arthur's teeth came out. They fascinated him. He drank and drank; he loved the taste. He watched his father die and drop from his arms.

When he came downstairs, Arthur said, "Let's see what we can do with our new power!"

The five of us went outside. The moon was full.

"I can now see so clearly," said Arthur. "It is so bright."

"We've told you basically what you need to know about being a vampire," said Edmond. "Now we will teach you how to fly."

"Do what we do," I said. "Let me demonstrate."

It was just like I was learning all over again. It was fun watching them learn, just doing circles in the air.

"We should go, children," said Edmond. "It is getting light out."

We flew home. "This is where you sleep, in the same coffins you woke up in. You three will learn more tomorrow."

They stepped into their coffins. They closed the lids themselves.

"See you at nightfall. Your mother and I will teach you new things."

Then we went into our own coffins. My eyes closed as the sun rose. I had my family now, forever.

When they awoke, we taught them how to feed without killing.

Dahlia stayed with us after the children became vampires, and until her natural death. We had offered her the choice to become a vampire. She decided against it, but was loyal to the end. We took care of her like she was family–because she was.

Annabelle, Josephine, and Arthur stayed with us for a while, then traveled from country to country. They met other people, made friends. They even fell in love, but the people they fell in love with didn't want to change, so they came home again, to the immortals who loved them.

Another 200 years passed. We lived good lives. But times change.

Edmond and I had many good years together with our family. I wouldn't have changed anything.

Still, we knew it was time to leave again. Edmond and I had bought a house in Greece. We planned to move there soon–people were getting suspicious of the family. But we were comfortable, and when you get comfortable you can put yourself in danger.

We were approaching our 400th year together. When that anniversary arrived, our life would change forever. It was a night I would never forget.

CHAPTER 5

You have to do this

After the five of us had fed and were flying home, a man followed us. The sun was going to rise soon. If it had been midnight, we'd have been stronger.

"I know who you people are–if you can be called people at all," he taunted us.

"Who are you, and why are you following us?" asked Edmond. (I should note here that by this time we were speaking the English you know from Chaucer. If I wrote it now verbatim, you'd not understand it all, though you'd get the gist. It's easier than Beowulf.)

We could see light in the sky.

"Who I am doesn't matter. It's what I am. I've been following you five for months, beginning when I saw the younger ones fly. I am a vampire hunter."

"Darling children, go inside now. I will take care of him."

Annabelle, Josephine, Arthur, and I ran inside, feeling relief from the sun. Our eyes were starting to close when we heard Edmond scream. We reached our coffins. I barred the door. I knew we were safe. I knew Edmond was dead.

I awoke instantly when the sun set. I sat motionless as I tried to take in what happened yesterday.

"Mother, Father died protecting us," said Annabelle, trying to comfort me. "We would also be dead if he hadn't fought him. There was not enough time. The sun was too bright."

"I know, Annabelle. I just don't know why we couldn't sense the hunter."

"He must have a strong mind," said Arthur. "He knows vampires' habits."

Gathering my wits, I said, "We must pack and leave this place. He is bound to come back. Vampire hunters never stop. I will get even with him though. He is going to die one night, and won't know who killed him. I have to get my family jewels."

"What family jewels, Mother?" asked Arthur.

"I took most of our jewels, the day before I died."

I showed the jewels to the children. "This is your family heritage now. You three are all I have left. I am never going to let anyone hurt you."

We left that night, locking the castle tight, knowing we could get back in anytime. There are ways known only to us. We flew up in the sky, looking down at our old home. There had been good times in that castle.

We flew to Greece, to the house Edmond and I had purchased.

Right after we landed, Josephine bumped into a man. "Oh, I'm sorry," he said. "Can I help you pick your bag up?"

"Thank you, but I can get it."

"My name is Alexander. What are you doing in Corinth?"

"I'm Josephine. This is Solena and Arthur and Annabelle."

We went inside to leave Josephine and Alexander alone. I knew that look.

"We have recently moved here," she said to him. "My father died not long ago, and we wanted to get away from where it happened."

"I'm very sorry. How did it happen, if you care to tell me?"

"He was killed. It isn't easy right now. Mother is taking care of us. She is very strong. I'm sorry, but I'm hungry and tired."

"May I take you somewhere?"

"I have what I need inside. I will eat with my family. But I will take a walk with you tomorrow. I love looking at the moon."

"You read my mind! I was going to ask you. I've never met a woman like you before."

"That has to do with my parents. They raised us to be strong. You will be surprised what you learn about me. I am not the normal woman."

"Tomorrow night then. Around seven o'clock?"

"Let's make it later. Two o'clock?"

"That sounds pretty late, but it is fine. I'll pick you up here."

"Please don't come during the day. I will be out."

Josephine was smiling when she walked into the house. "I just met the most wonderful man!"

The next night Josephine sat on the beach just outside our house, looking at the moon. She was wearing clothes proper to Greece.

"There you are! I see you are dressed differently."

"It is colder in England."

They walked hand in hand, then with arms around each other, all night, just walking. They didn't say anything. The communication was silent.

When it was nearing sunrise, Josephine said, "Alexander, I have to go home now."

"Why?"

"I just do. I can't explain now. I promise I will when it is time. Please don't ask me about it."

"Shall I see you again?"

"Yes, Alexander, certainly. You may stop by tomorrow evening, but after eight."

Josephine ran home, as she felt the deadly sun rising.

"Josephine, you scared us!"

"I'm sorry, Mother. It won't happen again."

"I understand. It's called 'young love.'"

"No, it is not! I'm tired. I need to go to bed."

Josephine and I walked downstairs together, just missing the sun's rays in the house's open parts. We got into our coffins, closed the lids, and went to sleep. I knew she was in love, even though she didn't admit it yet. I hoped he would accept her as she is.

When I slept, I dreamed of Edmond. I remembered how I first met him, my experience of "young love." I missed him so much, but it was nice seeing love happen to someone else I loved. It made up for some of the loss I felt.

I had something else on my mind, too–flying back to England to kill the vampire hunter. Edmond's death required revenge, and soon.

When we woke up, I told the children, "Tonight I'm leaving. I have some business to take care of. I'm going back to England to find Edmond's killer."

I changed into warm clothes. As I flew away, I saw Josephine meet Alexander. I was happy for her, but my mind was on other things.

Two days later I landed near the castle just in time to see the hunter. I tried to read his mind, but he was strong. He had known I would come back, so he blocked his thought from being read by anyone.

The sun was coming up. We had made some spaces outside the castle where we could sleep in emergencies. You can open them from the outside, but once you're in, they can be opened only from inside. In other words, I was safe.

At night, when I came out, I saw the hunter leaving. I followed him from the air, making sure he couldn't see me.

I waited until he was sleeping, then I attacked him. It was stupid of him to go to sleep. I went into his house and put him in a trance. When he woke up, he was scared. I bit into his neck, and drank my sweet revenge until he was dead. The wounds disappeared from his neck. I didn't know his wife was pregnant.

"Mother, you are home so soon!" exclaimed Arthur.

He and I took a walk. We saw Josephine and Alexander.

"Those two are in love," I said.

"Yes, I know. Josephine simply doesn't know it yet. He joined us last evening. We had a good time. I just hope I can find someone. When I watch those two together, I miss the girls I left."

Time passed. Josephine and Alexander kept seeing each other. I would see him running out of her room with fading teeth marks on his neck. When I asked her about it, she told me to leave her alone. I warned her not to endanger us. "I know what I'm doing," she said.

One night, about midnight, I spotted Josephine and Alexander on the cliff above the beach.

"Josephine, what's wrong?" he asked.

"Nothing, Alexander." She kissed him.

They started to sit on the ground, but Alexander stopped.

"Now, what's wrong with you?" asked Josephine.

"You're not telling me something."

She tried to kiss him again, but he pushed her away.

"Tell me what is wrong," he pleaded. "I want to know. I love you, and I don't like to see you hurt."

"I'm not hurt. But I've been thinking about something, and I have to tell you. I am among the undead. Now, don't be scared."

"What are you saying? You are a vampire? They don't exist!"

"Yes, they do. You are looking at one. My whole family is dead. Everyone in that house."

"I don't believe you."

"I will prove it to you."

I made my canine teeth come out.

"What are those?"

"They are my teeth that I use to drink blood."

Alexander got up and ran. Josephine flew up in the air and landed in front of him.

"You flew! How did you do that?"

"I told you. I'm a vampire."

He turned around and ran the other way, while continuing to look at her.

"Alexander, watch out for the cliff!"

He didn't hear Josephine. Alexander fell of the cliff to the rocky beach.

Josephine screamed. I ran to the window. Annabelle and Arthur ran into my room.

"Mother, what happened?"

"I don't know. You two stay here. I will go and find out."

I flew out the window. Josephine was already down on the beach, holding Alexander in her arms.

"I told him I am a vampire, and he ran from me. He didn't see the cliff. Mother, I love him! I don't want him to die."

His color was leaving him. "Josephine, he is dying."

"No, he can't, Mother."

Slowly, Alexander was coming to.

"Josephine, I love you, and I believe you. I don't hate you, no matter what you are."

Alexander saw me. He smiled, and once again lost consciousness.

"Josephine, if you want to be with him, you know what to do."

"But Mother, we don't have anything ready."

"This has to be done before he dies, or it won't work. You can do it, Josephine. I have faith in you. If you want to be with him, you have to do this."

She bent her head down toward his neck, and bit into it. The sweet blood flowed into her mouth as tears fell from her eyes. She grew stronger as he grew weaker.

Josephine withdrew her teeth, tore part of her dress to expose her breast, and picked up a sharp rock with which she cut her skin. The blood dripped into Alexander's mouth. Josephine bent down, and he pressed his lips to the cut.

I stepped back, to give them some privacy. I thought of Edmond.

Josephine stopped Alexander from drinking, and the wound closed. She picked him up, flew to the house, and went down to the crypt. She placed him in a coffin that was in the family's house and closed the lid. Then she came upstairs.

"Josephine, are you all right?" asked Annabelle.

"I just killed the man I love. But I am happy to have him forever– if he chooses to stay with me."

"I'm sure he'll choose to stay," said Arthur.

"I don't know. He ran from me when he found out what we are. Alexander didn't believe me at first."

"Josephine, we don't know what will happen until nightfall," I interjected. "I have to find him a first victim now. I will be back before sunrise."

Before I left, I saw the children going to their rooms. It was the right thing to do. Josephine wanted to be alone.

I got back a little before sunrise. I brought the boy to a cell we had built. I went down to bed. Josephine was looking at Alexander.

"Josephine, let him sleep. It is time for us to go to bed also."

"I know, Mother. I hope he accepts this condition."

"If he doesn't, he will have to die today. Let's go to bed."

We shut the door, and went to sleep.

CHAPTER 6

Life, or death ... whatever you want to call it

Alexander didn't know where he was. It was a dark, confined space. But what was strange–he could sense a lot of things around him. He was in a box made of stone, but with a soft bottom. His head was on a pillow. The lid was heavy, and he was surprised he could lift it.

It was pitch dark, but he could see. He tried to remember what happened. He was on the cliff with Josephine. She told him she was a vampire. He remembered falling off the cliff. He saw Josephine and Solena. He said he believed her.

Then this very vague recollection–a sharp pain in his neck. After the pain, he was seeing memories and the future. Then he was drinking something, wanting more but not getting any.

He stepped out of the box, and saw it was a coffin. For the first time, he noticed he wasn't breathing, and there was no air in the room. He opened the door and sucked air into his lungs. But he realized he didn't need it.

He followed the hallway and climbed a flight of stairs. He opened the door, and when he closed it it seemed to disappear. He knew he was at Josephine's house. She walked into the room with Solena.

"We were wondering when you would rise."

"Josephine, what did you do to me?"

"I saved your life, Alexander. You'd have died if I hadn't done what I did."

"What exactly did you do?"

"I turned you into a vampire."

"She made you one of us out of love for you," I added.

"Out of love? How can this be 'out of love'? You don't kill somebody when you love them!"

I left at that point, to join my other children.

"I didn't exactly kill you. You are still alive, sort of. And I did it because I love you. You now have eternal life."

"But I don't want eternal life!"

"You can still die, if you want. Starve yourself, or stay in the sun."

Alexander ran out, and Josephine burst into tears. I heard her crying and came to see what happened,

"Mother, he ran out. He hates me now."

"He doesn't hate you. He will come back, because he loves you, or at least because of the hunger. Becoming a vampire without wanting it is a big shock. If he comes back, it will be tonight. He knows this is the only safe place."

Annabelle and Arthur also assured Josephine that everything would be all right, but she wasn't persuaded.

Alexander hurried home. He went up to his bedroom and took off his clothes, bloodstained from the fall. He saw himself in the mirror. His skin was pale, and there was a new beauty, like that of Josephine and her family.

He put on new clothes and went downstairs to get something to eat. When he tried to swallow the food, he couldn't, and spit it out.

Then he smelled the most wonderful aroma. It was blood. It was his mother's blood; he could see it pulsing through her veins. He ran out of the house before she saw him.

He ran into the street and grabbed a beggar. He pushed him around the corner. He felt his teeth come out. He bit into the man's neck, and drank until he was dead. Alexander was shocked by what he had done, but he also liked it.

He carried the man's body to the ocean. He couldn't believe how strong he was; the body seemed light as a feather.

Alexander ran back to Josephine's house, amazed that he arrived there so quickly. Annabelle, Arthur, and I looked at him; we didn't have to say a thing. We got up to leave.

He walked up to Josephine, who was by the window, looking at the ocean.

"Josephine."

"Alexander, why are you here? I thought you had rejected me."

"I did at first. But I realized I couldn't live without you."

"When?" she said, not looking at him.

"When I killed a beggar tonight. I found out how precious life is. And how life could be taken away just like that."

"So you understand why I brought you into the realm of the undead?"

"Yes, out of love."

He took hold of her waist and turned her towards him.

"Josephine, I want to be with you in any condition."

He pulled her closer to him and kissed her. She took a tight hold on his waist, and jumped up. She flew out the window, with Alexander floating behind, and landed on the beach.

"How did you do that?"

"Come, Alexander, let me show you the wonderful gift I have given you."

She let go of him and jumped up in the air. She stayed stationary.

"Alexander, come to me!"

"How do I?"

"Jump up in the air and think you want to stay up."

She blew him a kiss for luck. He flew over to her. They both took off and flew higher and higher.

"What if someone sees us?"

"They can't. We are safe. There is a reason my parents bought this house."

"How do we land?"

"All you need to do is think about it. But don't land over water."

"Will the water harm us?"

"No, but it isn't fun to land in."

After they had alighted, Josephine said, "You probably know how strong you are."

"I found that out tonight." He picked up a big rock and threw it into the sea.

Josephine and Alexander ran along the beach, enjoying life, or death. Whatever you want to call it.

They dropped down on the sandy beach, the waves splashing over them. They made love in the moonlight. Alexander had never experienced anything like it before.

His lips kissed her neck. He could smell her blood. His teeth came out. He bit into her neck. As he bit, she arched her back in pleasure. She stood up, while holding him tight. She jumped up in the air, forced him away from her neck, and bit into his. They slowly spiraled to the ground as she drank his blood. They lay on the sand, resting.

"Josephine."

"Yes."

"Will you marry me?"

"With all my heart!"

They lay there for hours. Then Josephine noticed that the sky was getting lighter.

"Alexander, we have to go in now."

"Why? It is so beautiful out here!"

"The sun will rise soon, and that will kill us."

Alexander had started to feel the heat, because he was newly dead. "You don't have to tell me why, because I can feel it."

They flew home, through the window they had left from earlier.

"We were getting worried about you two," I said.

"We have some news for you," said Josephine. "Alexander has asked me to marry him, and I have said yes."

"Do you know about the vampire marriage ceremony?" I asked.

"No, we don't. Please tell us."

"Two vampires getting married must both drink from the same victim at the same time. The victim must die, and the body must be burned at midnight. Only when you have done exactly this can you start your life together as vampires. It was different for me and Edmond. I was human when we married."

"May we do it soon, Mother?"

"Only on a full moon and clear night. It is tough to be married by vampire standards!"

"We accept those standards," replied Alexander.

The sun was rising. We had to go to bed.

When I awoke, they had already gone. Josephine was teaching Alexander how to feed without killing.

I went out to feed, and to find a sacrificial victim for the wedding. I also picked up a special gown for Josephine and a suit for Alexander. The traditional wedding dress for vampires is blood red—I would have to dye the two outfits with animal blood.

The moon would be full in a few nights, so the wedding would take place soon.

I remembered a wedding Edmond and I came upon in Spain, where the victim was on a table, fully awake and aware of what was happening, but couldn't move or speak. This reminded me I would have to put together some sort of table in the yard and gather wood for a big fire. We would probably burn the body on the beach.

When I got home, Josephine and Alexander were back. I went outside to find an animal to kill, so I could dye the new clothes.

"Josephine."

"Yes, Alexander."

"What did you see when you were changed? I saw the future, and you were in it."

"Well, I hope I am in it! I saw the past and future. Like when our parents kicked us out. I didn't see Edmond die, or my parents die, either. I saw you. I wondered who you were. Then I recognized you when we met. But I only saw a little bit of you.

"Alexander, the moon is going to be full soon. We are going to have to decide if we want to stay here or move to another place. There are places we can go."

"I want to stay here with your family for a while, and I would like to see England too."

"I'd love to show you England! I hope you have warmer clothes. This reminds me, we should get your clothes. You can't stay at your home anymore. People get very suspicious."

"Will I be able to see my parents again?"

"I don't know. Our safety is very important."

"I will say goodbye to them tonight, then."

They went to his house, gathered his clothes, and bid farewell to his parents.

On the way back, Alexander asked, "How are we to dress for our wedding?"

"My mother is taking care of that. I don't really know. I've never been to a vampire wedding."

They saw me placing a stone table in the yard.

"Mother, what is that for?"

"This is the sacrifice table. It is high enough for you two to stand while drinking. If even one thing is wrong, the marriage isn't valid. The moon will be full in a couple of days. I've also been preparing your proper dress for a vampire wedding."

"What are they?"

"You will find out soon enough, Josephine. You two are not to feed that night, before the ceremony."

The night of the wedding arrived. There was a big pile of sticks on the beach, and torches were lit in the yard. Our house was far enough from town for nobody to notice. And I had a human on guard. We kept him on after the wedding, so our house was safely guarded ever since that night.

I awoke earlier than the rest of the house. When others were up, Josephine asked, "What do we need to do to get ready?"

"There are clothes in your room, and Alexander's are in the room next to it."

I walked upstairs with them, and went into Alexander's room.

"You may call me Mother if you want."

"I like Solena. I have a mother, even though I have said goodbye to her."

"That is hard to do. When I did it, we burned down the house. My parents thought we died."

Alexander looked at the clothes. "What color is this?"

"Blood red. From an animal. Josephine's dress is the same color. We aren't vicious killers, but we do this to maintain that death occurs when we become vampires. It makes it more real for us."

"So this is why we kill, Solena?"

"Yes. It is like marriage by blood. I have to go help Josephine, and then prepare the victim. By the way, I am honored to have you for a son-in-law. You are a good person, or vampire."

Josephine was already dressed when I entered her room.

"Mother, how is this dress colored? I am nervous."

"So was I when I married your father. You will do fine."

"This dress is soft. When blood dries, it hardens."

"Not the way I did it. I mixed the blood with an oil. I must go down now. Annabelle and Arthur are dressing for tonight."

I left to change, and then to get the victim from the cell he was in. I took him to the yard and tied him on the table. Then I gave him instructions. Once he had them, I untied him. I took him out of the first trance to tell him the second instructions. The man lay still on the table, tied down not by rope but by thought.

Alexander and Josephine came out of the house. They walked to the table. The man saw them, was scared, but couldn't get up. They could smell fear in his blood.

Their teeth came out. Alexander and Josephine both bent down and bit into his neck. They felt united, forever.

Once married, vampires are united until death. Otherwise, they have to save a life together. Marriage is taking a life, divorce is giving a life on purpose. This may sound strange to you, but not for vampires.

When the man died, they stopped. We all danced around the table and celebrated.

At midnight Alexander and Josephine picked up the body. I took a torch. We walked down the path to the beach and placed the corpse on the pile of sticks. I gave the torch to them. Annabelle, Arthur, and I watched as they set the man on fire.

When he was completely burned, we all flew back to the house. Alexander and Josephine went into a room and did what newlyweds do.

I stayed downstairs with Annabelle and Arthur. When it was time to go into our coffins, the young newlyweds came down. We had all changed. I had burned all our wedding clothes. This is what you do.

We went to bed with a new family member, and a very happy daughter and sister.

CHAPTER 7

We can spare one human

After the wedding, Alexander and Josephine went away to England, where they lived for a year or two, then came back to Greece. Alexander didn't want to leave the place he was born, and Josephine didn't want to leave us.

Years passed, and we did more traveling, but we kept coming back to that home.

We were in the fifteenth century now.

One evening I was walking on the beach. I had just finished talking with Annabelle, who had asked me what happened when I went back to England all those years ago, and I had told her.

Alone on the beach, I saw a vampire flying in the air. She was going to land in our yard, but she saw me, and alighted on the beach.

"Solena, I finally found you!"

"Christina, what are you doing here?"

She walked up and hugged me. "I'm so happy to see you. You've been gone a long time."

"I'm happy to see you, too. What a surprise! Please come in."

We flew up the cliff.

"It's even more beautiful now than the last time I was here."

"You must be hot. Come, I will get you some decent clothes."

"I didn't think to bring the proper clothes. You see, I didn't know where you were."

"What is so urgent that you had to see me?"

"I've been flying to every house of yours I know of. This was my last resort."

We went into the living room and sat down.

"Vampires have been dying all over England."

"How is this possible? I took care of the hunter."

"His wife was pregnant when you killed him. She had twins. The girl turned out to be normal. The boy has been the problem. He has been killing us."

"How do you know it is him?"

"I have seen him kill, just before sunrise. Just like his father did. He goes back when the sun is up, and sleeps."

"How sly! Have you found out where he lives?"

"No, he has a mind stronger even than his father's. He must be killed at night. But vampires have tried and died. In the middle of the night even."

"How does he do this?"

"He uses fire. Puts a torch to their clothing. And you know what happens; it's not just our clothes that burn. Or he corners us just before sunrise. So, we've left the area where he is. Several vampires are sharing lairs with vampires who don't have spare houses. We must save the English vampires."

"What can I do?"

"You will go with us to kill him."

"How can I, if others haven't been able to?"

"I don't know. We have to figure out something."

"I'm game."

Just then Alexander and Josephine walked in.

"Mother, who is this?"

"This is an old friend from when I was mortal. She lives in England."

"My name is Christina. You must be Josephine. Solena and Edmond have talked a lot about you. Is this Arthur?"

"No, this is my husband, Alexander."

"And when did this happen?"

"About thirty years ago."

"Was it a traditional vampire wedding?"

"Oh yes, of course. It could be nothing else."

"You two knew each other when you were mortal?" Alexander asked.

"Sit down, we will tell you the story," I said.

"Then I would like to hear how you two met," added Christina. "Oh, by the way, where are the other children?"

Annabelle walked in.

"And you are Annabelle?"

"Who is this?"

"This is my friend from when I was mortal. She is of course like us now."

"I was going to tell how we met," said Christina. "Sit down and join us.

"We were childhood friends. I was from a poor family. One day we met in town. We were about ten years old. We then spent lots of time together."

"I'll add a detail," I said. "Our cook was doing the shopping, and we came across Christina begging. We gave her some food."

"My mother got very upset with me. She made me repay Solena's family for the food. They wouldn't accept the few pence

I had to repay them with, but they invited me to have supper with them. They were the lords of the town.

"I accepted the invitation. When I got home, my mother was even angrier with me. We went to Wilshire Manor together. She was going to make me pay them back, with her there. When she talked to Lord and Lady Wilshire, they said they wanted Solena to have a friend."

"I didn't really have a lot of friends," I interjected. "When your family has that sort of position, other parents think 'Our kids are getting charity,' and they resent it."

"Times haven't changed, even in centuries. I often walk in town. I see this all the time. Solena's family, generations farther along, still going by the name Wilshire, still being begrudged.

"With her parents' blessing, Solena and I became best friends. I stayed many nights at Wilshire Manor. Your mother's house was my second home.

"I was at her wedding. Her death shocked me. The whole town thought she and Edmond had died. Little did we know they were already dead.

"I died a few years later. It was by a stranger. She made me and disappeared. When I was discovering what it was like to be a vampire, I came upon Solena when I was walking in the woods. When I saw her, I was shocked."

"Shocked? She fainted!" I said. "We carried her inside, or else the sun would have killed her. The next night she told me about my funeral, and about what was going on in the world."

"They said I could stay with them for a while. I was a new vampire. I had much to learn. Eventually I found a new home.

"Solena and Edmond let me know when they found you two and your brother, and said they didn't want other vampires around just then. When I heard they had changed the three of you, I left the country and stayed away for a long time. I traveled the world.

"I never got to meet you. But I have been to nearly every house Solena owns, just missing you along with her other friends."

"We wanted to keep you away from us," I said. "It is nice to have friends, but we wanted you to make your own. You have met other vampires?"

"I have met one in my most recent travels," said Christina.

"Why did you come?" asked Alexander.

"Vampires are dying in England, by the son of the man who killed Edmond. I have come here to ask Solena's help in killing him."

"You are going to kill him, Solena?"

"Alexander, one of us must die. I have accepted that, and I am not going to be the one to die. We are going to work together."

"So vampires kill when there is need? Just like in the wedding ceremony?"

"Yes, just like anybody else," said Christina. "Don't be so astonished. It is them or else. There are more humans than vampires. We can spare one human to save our race. And how did you become a vampire, Alexander?"

"I fell from a cliff when Josephine told me she was a vampire. So, to save my life, she changed me. Josephine has even taken me to England. We stayed in the castle she lived in for over 200 years."

"I wasn't sure he was going to accept being a vampire," said Josephine, "but these have been good centuries. When are you two going to be leaving, Mother?"

"I don't know. We have to figure out what to do. Christina tells me he is tough."

Alexander and Josephine left, so Christina and I could plan. I told her I had an idea.

We left for England the next night. We found the hunter lurking around the castle I had lived in. I walked up to him, while Christina quietly walked behind him.

"Hello," I said, "I know you."

"And I know you. You are the vampire who killed my father!"

"I have no idea what you're talking about."

"My mother described you from what my father told her you look like, the night he died."

"All right, I admit it. But your father killed my husband."

"So that is why you killed him! But vampires deserve to die."

"We don't hurt people. We're just trying to survive."

"You do hurt people. I've seen you kill them. I've seen ceremonies. You are vicious creatures."

I forced my fangs out.

"We may be vicious, but when forced."

I lunged toward him. He brought his torch toward me. I jumped back a little.

"You are why I have been hunting. I am going to kill you tonight."

"No, you aren't."

When I said that, Christina jumped on him. The torch fell to the ground. She bit into his neck. He struggled, but she was too strong for him. I watched as Christina drank his blood.

We burned his body. With two vampires, it was easier. We vowed to keep track of that family, because it could happen again. I was a target for them.

But others would be safe. Christina made sure other vampires knew they could go home.

I scattered the hunter's ashes on the ocean on my way back to Greece.

CHAPTER 8

... Though he left out the vampire part

Trouble was starting in Greece. The Turks. They were invading every city.

We had already decided to leave, but we did so sooner than we had planned. We didn't want people to be suspicious, but they had started. Arthur had come back a couple of months before. He was alarmed to see the Turks.

We moved back to England. This time we stayed in the castle where Edmond died, until another place could be built. The new house wasn't as big as the castle; we didn't need that much room. But we installed extra coffins, just in case.

Christina was happy to see us, and finally to meet Arthur.

While the house was being built, Arthur went to Egypt. He loved the last city he saw, Alexandria. The sights were just amazing.

When I talk about the sights, it's not buildings. It's Jessica.

Her father was Egyptian, but her mother was whiter than most people there, so Jessica had uncommonly fair skin.

Arthur saw her walking home as he came out for the evening. Her long, flowing hair blew in the wind. It was love at first sight. He followed her home, then he found supper.

This was his second night in Alexandria, and he hadn't yet found proper shelter. He went to an inn. Vampires always bring money with them, even if they don't need it. He paid the innkeeper a little, in a way to make it seem like the full amount.

Arthur got a room in the basement with no window. He sealed the crack between the door and the floor. He used the bed. The day before he had slept in the sand, with his belongings in a bag.

The next night he got up, fed, and then went to find the girl he saw earlier, whose name he wished he knew. He went to her house. It clearly belonged to a rich family.

She came outside. He followed her. She went into a restaurant, and so did he. He sat down at a table. The smell of food made him sick, but the smell of blood made him hungry. He ordered water, knowing full well he couldn't drink it. He watched Jessica from a distance, and finally made his move.

"Pardon me, miss; I have been noticing your beauty."

"What?"

"Oh, I'm sorry. Did I offend you?"

"No, you just startled me. That's all."

"My name is Arthur, and I have been wanting to meet you."

Her friends were giggling. She told them to be quiet.

"Hello, Arthur. My name is Jessica. I'm glad someone thinks I'm beautiful."

"You mean you don't think you are?"

"Well, of course I do!"

Arthur looked into her eyes and asked her to come with him. She stood up and left with him, to her friends' amazement. They actually tried to stop her, but she didn't listen to them.

"Arthur, why am I going with you?"

"Because I want you to. But you are welcome to go back and join your friends if you want to."

Arthur stopped his trance on her, but she stayed with him. They walked, talking, in the city's streets. A couple of hours later they had reached her house. "I will see you tomorrow night," he said.

He showed up, just as he said he would. Jessica wasn't surprised.

While they were sitting in a swing in the garden, she read him poems she had written. She explained about her family.

Her mother had died a couple of years ago, but before she died, she brought Jessica to her father. "My mother was a slave; her skin color was light. She was going to leave the country; that's why she brought me to my father–she wanted her daughter to be safe. But she died before she could leave. I love my father very much."

Arthur told Jessica about his family, though he left out the vampire part. He explained that his real parents kicked them out, and that Edmond and I brought them in. He also told her that Edmond had died and they now live in England and, lying, that he was here in Egypt on business.

They kept seeing each other. Arthur always came to pick her up, at night. Jessica wanted to know more about him.

So, one night after Arthur had walked her home, she followed him. Now she knew where he lived. Just before sunset, she went there, and when Arthur came out she followed him. He had no idea she was there. She wasn't on his mind. He only wanted to eat.

He found a child, apparently close to teen age, separated from his mother. Arthur walked up to him, put him in a trance, and bit into his neck. Jessica watched from the corner, horrified. She thought the boy was going to die. She was going to do something, but then Arthur stopped. The boy walked away, not knowing what had happened.

Jessica ran home. She had no idea what to do. She now knew what he was, but she loved him, and was sure he wouldn't hurt her.

She decided to confront him about the fact that he was a vampire.

It wasn't especially strange that she knew what to call him. In those days, belief in vampires was widespread. Premature burial, normal body decomposition, and plague all fed into the stories people told.

When Arthur came to pick her up, she said she wanted to talk to him.

"Jessica, what is it?"

"I saw something very disturbing tonight."

"What did you see?"

"I saw you."

"What do you mean, you saw me?"

"I saw you eat supper."

At that point she pulled out a cross (there are Christians in Egypt). Arthur backed away from her.

"Arthur, don't run away. Please stay. I will put the cross away."

Arthur came closer, knowing full well she could pull the cross out again.

"Arthur, I know you are a vampire. I saw you drink from that boy. If you had killed him, I'd have intervened, but you didn't. I know you won't hurt me, but I brought the cross, just in case. You can never be too careful!"

"You aren't scared? I drink blood, and only blood."

"No, I'm not, because I know you. Was Josephine's husband scared when he found out?"

"How did you know my whole family are vampires?"

"Because it makes sense that vampires hang out together, now that I know they live as close to normal lives as possible. I saw that in you. I bet your parents were vampires when you three came to them."

"You are right. Well, I guess I will be leaving soon."

"Why will you go?"

"Because you know what I am."

"Why does that mean you can't stay?"

"I may be in danger now. I am leaving for my own safety. I'm not going to hurt you. I love you!"

"What? You love me?"

"Yes! I have loved you from the first moment I saw you, Jessica. That is why I wanted to meet you. And I don't want to see you hurt. Vampire hunters will kill you to get to me. Lately I've had the feeling that I'm being watched."

"That was me. I followed you last night, and tonight."

"No, I had this feeling before. Almost since my first night in Alexandria. I didn't have this feeling in other cities of Egypt."

"Can I come with you?"

"Why do you want to do that?"

"I want to be with you."

"I flew here."

"Flew? How do you do that?"

"I'm a vampire. And no, I don't turn into a bat."

"How did you know I was going to ask that?"

"The most common question! My mother asked my father that before she changed."

"What do you mean, 'changed'?"

"Before he turned her into a vampire."

"And how do you do that?"

"It's privileged information. Only people who are transformed can find out."

"Well, I would like to find out."

"Only if we ever come to that point. Being a vampire isn't all that great. I miss things. Human things. Like food. And watching sunrises."

"I would still like to come with you."

"What about your father? Won't you miss him?"

"Of course I would, but for some time I have wanted to leave this country. How would I get over there to England?"

"I could carry you as I fly. I'm very strong. But you would have to find something to do as I rested during the day."

"We could travel the world on our way there!"

"Just a minute! I never said I would take you with me. I do love you, but I don't know about this."

"I'm taking the risk, not you."

"I'm sorry. I can't do this to you."

Arthur walked away, crying. Jessica ran after him. But he jumped up in the air and flew away. Jessica went home. Arthur went back to the inn to collect his things. He didn't leave that night. There wasn't enough night left.

Jessica knew what she had to do. She figured out that Arthur would probably leave the next night. She gathered money and a few clothes, and told her father she was going to travel.

She went to the inn. The sun had just set. Arthur came out.

"Jessica, what are you doing here?"

"I'm going to England, one way or another. If you aren't going to take me, I will take a boat and find you. You can't stop me."

"Yes, I can."

"You won't stop me."

"You're right. You can come with me. It's safer to fly with me than to go on a ship. Let me eat first. Wait here. I will be back. Do you have some food?"

"Yes, I do. I didn't bring a lot of stuff."

"That's good. We don't want to be too heavy."

Arthur went to eat, then came back. He also had a thick rope with him. He tied it around his waist, then around Jessica's waist and shoulders. He made sure the knot was secure.

"What is this for, Arthur?"

"So you are safe. Do you think you will be warm enough in the air?"

"I think I will, or I will at least handle it."

"Let's go!"

Arthur jumped up. They flew away.

They flew in silence. They had to land when Arthur saw the sky getting lighter. They landed, and Arthur slept during the day. England wasn't that far away.

Arthur contacted me via thought. He wondered whether the house was finished. I told him it was, and its exact location. He and Jessica landed a couple of hours after midnight.

We were surprised that someone was with him. He saw the four of us waiting–and wanting an explanation.

"Welcome back, Arthur. And who is this?" I asked.

"This is Jessica. I met her in Egypt, in Alexandria."

"Does she know?"

"Yes, Annabelle. Or else she wouldn't be here. She wanted to see England."

"But Arthur, this is so dangerous!"

"Mother, she won't hurt us. I'm sure of it."

"I know I can trust you. So I suppose I can trust her."

"Jessica, my name is Annabelle. This is my sister, Josephine, and her husband Alexander."

"How nice to meet all of you! I have heard so much about you."

"And my name is Solena. Welcome to our home. Arthur, how was your trip?"

"I thought it would be harder to fly with someone else, but it wasn't."

"Jessica, please come in."

"Thank you, Solena. Considering the circumstances, it is strange I am welcome the way I am."

"If Arthur trusts you, we can," said Josephine.

Arthur and Jessica got a grand tour of the house, and a listing of the house rules for mortals. She strictly followed those rules.

Jessica disappeared when we went to bed, so she had no idea where we slept. She and Arthur spent a lot of the night together, exploring England.

She stayed close to a year. I knew she and Arthur were getting serious. I decided to talk to Arthur.

"Are you and Jessica going out tonight?"

"No, we plan to stay in."

"Good, I have to talk to you."

"What about, Mother?"

"About Jessica. How long is she going to stay here?"

"I don't know."

"I'm worried. She is easy to get to by hunters. They catch on to situations quite fast."

"So you think we are in danger?"

"No, I don't. Not yet."

"What do you mean?"

"You have to make a decision. If you want to be with Jessica for any longer, you are going to have to offer her immortality."

"I want to, but I don't think it is time. I want to be with her forever, but I don't know if she wants to stay with me."

"She does. I can see it. If you want to marry her, ask her. I can almost guarantee she will say yes, if that's what you want to do. If not, she will have to leave soon. Our house is too close to town. You must make up your mind soon."

"I know. I probably will. It is forever with us. I'm just scared. I'll do it. Tonight. I feel better now."

"Jessica's coming. I will leave you two alone. Remember, if you get married you have the option of both weddings. And if she says no, she'll have to leave, and forget about us forever."

"I understand. These are the rules for vampires."

"Arthur, there you are," said Jessica. "I've been looking for you."

"Why?"

"I was wondering if you wanted to take a walk."

"Let me take you somewhere else instead."

"Where?"

"The castle I spent 200 years in. I want to show you where I changed. It is a special place for me."

Arthur picked her up and they left. It didn't take long to get there. He flew in and opened the door.

"Welcome to a special home of mine. This is where Josephine and Alexander spent their honeymoon. We died here, and were also born here at the same time. Let's sit down. I want to ask you something."

"What do you want to ask?"

Arthur stood up and walked around. He was very nervous.

"Arthur, please tell me what it is you want to ask me!"

"This is very hard. Well, here goes. Jessica?"

"Yes."

"I love you, and I want to be with you forever."

"I also want to be with you forever."

"This means I want to marry you. But there's a catch."

"What catch?"

"If you marry me, you must become a vampire."

"Can I think about this?"

"Of course. I will leave you alone for a while."

"Oh, please don't leave the castle, though."

"Of course not."

Arthur walked to a window and looked out. A little while later Jessica came up to him.

"I have made up my mind. I will marry you. I know there is sacrifice involved, but it is worth it."

"Jessica, I love you so much! Now we have a choice to make."

"And what is that?"

"Alexander didn't have the choice. I'm glad you do. You may become a vampire before or after the marriage."

"What's the difference?"

"The ceremony. If you stay human during it, it will be a normal wedding. But if you choose to become a vampire before, there is a vampire ceremony, which involves blood and the killing of a victim."

"Which way will we be truly married?"

"In my eyes, it is the vampire ceremony. It symbolizes everlasting life."

"I want that one, then."

"First we must go back home. I want you to be human one more day."

"Why?"

"I want you to remember what it is like."

Jessica soaked in every aspect of human life.

The moon would be full in about a week, so the change had to happen soon. The next night, Arthur bit into her neck, and after he stopped he cut open his neck and she drank. The next night she killed her first victim. It didn't bother her at all.

When the next full moon arrived it was cloudy, so the ceremony had to be postponed. I kept everything ready for the next full moon.

A month later our friends were at the wedding. Almost every English vampire was there. The bride and groom in their blood-soaked clothes were beautiful. We all danced around the victim's body. We were at the castle, where Arthur and Jessica spent their wedding night. But they didn't live there.

They continued to live with the rest of the family. Vampires want to be safe. People can't find us out unless they want to join us.

I continued to monitor the vampire hunter's family, with Christina's help. There was no activity for years.

The English vampires were safe, and had an active social life. People may not believe we have fun, but we do.

CHAPTER 9

That's not much of a legend

Time passed. (I should note that here and elsewhere in this memoir I include "time passed" for your benefit. From your perspective, "now" and "before" and "after," "years," "decades," "centuries," even "millennia" help orient you. Immortality, such as we vampires have, drains the calendar of most of its meaning. I can recall speaking different kinds of English in the tenth and fourteenth centuries, and I'll almost certainly use yet another kind in the twenty-fourth or thirtieth or hundredth, but at no point am I forced to say, "This is it." I will confess, however, that once in a very great while, and only momentarily, I think what a relief "This is it" would be. But immortality immediately reasserts itself.)

The Chemberlins, the family that had killed Edmond, moved to America in the 1800s. Just like so many other families. We came here to watch them.

The Chemberlins moved to New York, we to Boston.

The story that I killed one of their forefathers was passed on by word of mouth from generation to generation. They want me dead. In order to stay alive, I have to be smarter—which isn't too hard. And it is dangerous to hunt vampires these days. The authorities get involved.

So for now we were safe. We opened a clothing shop in Boston (we sold food and supplies too). There weren't too many night jobs in those days, so we were able to cater both to humans–during the day–and to vampires–at night.

One of our specialties was old-style clothing. If in a dream I am clothed as I was when I was alive, I feel a bit alive again. My kids, and our customers, felt the same way, and my kids still do. Of course, tenth-century fashion is not easy to come by!

Word of our products spread, and vampires came from all over Massachusetts.

We made more friends in America than we ever had in England. America was for us, as for so many, the land of opportunity.

Eventually the whole family moved to New York. I bought three buildings (with basements)–one for Arthur and Jessica, one for Josephine and Alexander, and the third for Annabelle and me. Everything was airtight. The windows were covered up. For the first time in our dead lives, we could sleep in beds. This, even now, makes me temporarily feel human.

Had humans entered our building, air could have come in. I have not yet explained the air deal.

Vampires don't speak with their vocal cords. Dead bodies can't speak. We speak through our minds, but the sound comes out through our mouths. It's hard to explain. We project the sound. We don't need air, but we can breathe, and we do around humans.

There are countless vampires in New York. I meet them just walking down the street. One of my new friends showed us a meeting spot, a hill overlooking the city. We of course meet when most people are asleep. Some of the friends I met there work for me today.

Soon we were in the twentieth century. I liked it when technology got better, but I still missed the time when I was alive.

Most people, especially in American cities, didn't believe in vampires anymore. The belief was strong–and still is–in villages in Europe. But the fact that in New York people and vampires both tend to go unnoticed meant we were safe.

In 1931 we went to see the new movie, "Dracula." We laughed about how little Bram Stoker knew–he didn't even know he was writing about a real thing!

As we were leaving the cinema, Annabelle literally bumped into another vampire. His name was Doug.

She had not been lucky in love. Dated just a little, but nothing serious.

She dropped her bag. Doug said, "I am so sorry. I did not see you."

"Oh, that's okay. No harm done."

"My name is Doug. Who may you be?"

"I am Annabelle. Nice to meet you."

The rest of us walked away and let them talk. We saw the look on Annabelle's face.

Doug came over to the house later that night.

Doug was new in town. He knew no vampires in the area. He was from Romania, where he'd become a vampire in the late 1800s.

Romania was not a safe place for vampires. Some people who lived in the country still believed in them and followed the customs of what to do: stake through the heart, cut the heart out and burn it, then drink the ashes.

Doug had gone to see "Dracula" because the setting reminded him of home.

Annabelle and Doug were together a lot. I was glad she met someone. It had been a long time since she was really happy.

The Depression was tough. We had transferred our business from Boston to New York. The vampire dealings were still good, but we needed the human commerce to stay afloat. I had family money left, but I had to save it; we had homes to maintain.

When the business went under, our vampire customers were disappointed. So we had to hunt during the Depression. There were many people on the streets, but we had to be careful. Back in Boston, it had been easier. We simply kept human customers in the shop a little longer.

During this time, since there was no business for them to work in, Josephine and Alexander moved back to Greece for a while, and Arthur and Jessica also took the opportunity to travel.

With the economic boom that followed World War II, I made a lot of money (got lucky in the stock market) and got into another business. Actually, I think of myself as a businesswoman. I am very independent, as I was when I was alive–as Edmond himself noticed the first time I met him.

I invested in another store, like the one I originally had in Boston. Some clients came back. But I don't operate the store anymore; I have hired a vampire to run it.

In the 1970s I started an escort service. It gave me an easier way to feed, and I needed a new interest anyway. I lived alone by that time. Annabelle had lived about forty years with her vampire boyfriend, Doug, but they still didn't want to get married.

To go about my new business, I went to the proper people for "protection." Everybody who needs to think it legal thinks it "legal."

I bought a building and rented the lower offices out. I didn't advertise. I contacted the rich, which New York has plenty of. The 1970s was the "me" decade. People wanted to please themselves, and I provided that service.

I have two types of employees–humans and vampires. Clients never have sex with any of my human employees. I don't allow it. I worry about what they can catch. I worried about it before the rest of the world did.

What people don't know is that I don't follow through on what they think is my business–sex. It is my vampire employees, and I and my family too, who "escort" the clients. It is a safe way for us to feed.

We don't have to sneak around. We do it in the privacy of specially designed rooms. We drink the clients' blood on a king-size bed. If the clients knew what we do, they would fear for their lives, but they aren't in any danger. They come out thinking they've had the best "sex" in their lives.

Women are included in the client list. I employ male vampires too. We all have to feed.

And believe me, my reputation spreads by word of mouth. There is a waiting list for the "sexual" services.

It's not cheap. The charge is $300 a night. I pay the vampires $100, so most of it is profit for me.

The human employees are escorts–which isn't illegal. Wealthy bachelors and bachelorettes look for dates for the evening. You would be amazed how many single, rich people are out there with no special person in their lives.

I spent more and more time on Vampire Hill. One day in 1976, when attending a vampire wedding up there, I met a very old soul. He reminded me of Edmond.

"What a beautiful wedding."

"What? I didn't catch what you said," I said.

"I didn't mean to surprise you."

"That's okay. I thought the wedding was lovely. What do you think?"

"I think I said that already."

"That's what you said? How funny that I would say the same thing! My name is Solena Wilshire."

"My name is Jonathan Anderson (call me 'John'). 'Wilshire.' Sounds like an old name. English, perhaps?"

"How did you guess? Yes, I'm from England. How about you?"

"I'm from Sweden. A Sweden many years ago."

"What a coincidence! I'm from an old England."

"How old of an England? I visited there about 800 years ago."

"What part of England?"

"I believe it was in the north. I stayed in the town of–come to think of it–Wilshire."

"My family were lords of the town!"

"Then was it you?"

"What do you mean?"

"A legend got started in that town."

"What kind of legend?"

"It is about a lord's daughter who died. A terrible death. She and her husband died in a fire–shortly after they were married. The family jewels disappeared."

"That's not much of a legend."

"I'm not finished. The town grieved for the woman, then went on with life. But a few years later a resident was coming home from a long trip. He came to a castle and thought he could sleep there. He was going to enter when he heard the door start to open. He hid behind a tree. A man walked out, then a woman. He had known her when she was alive–and that she had died. He had even attended her funeral!

"He didn't stop, but headed home, where he arrived a couple of days later. He told the lords what he had seen. The woman's parents traveled to the castle. They saw her, but didn't let her see them. To them, their daughter was dead. This was no longer their daughter.

"When they came back home, they said it was true. A woman was seen going into their house. Soon after, the parents fell ill. They died a couple of weeks later. The village had kept watch, but it didn't help. They blamed the parents' death on the daughter–who they knew was a vampire, since if she had come back from the dead, that's what she had to be. But she had burned to death. They couldn't make sense of it.

"So, they stayed away from the castle. Now they say it's haunted. So is the parents' bedroom, and the family that moved into their house sealed that room off and stopped going out at night."

"The people who moved into the house were the aunt and uncle, right?"

"How do you know that?"

"Because they were my aunt and uncle. I saw that when I died, but I don't remember seeing the part about my parents' death."

"So, it is you!"

"Yes, and I did not kill my parents. I wonder who did. Some vampires did stalk families and kill them."

"I have known vampires who do that. It gives us a bad name."

"I never thought this would happen. I wonder if the legend still stands? I wonder if the house still stands?"

"I don't know. But I wouldn't go back there if I were you."

"I know the castle still stands. We renovated it. It was falling apart."

"What happened to your husband?"

"He's dead."

"I'm sorry. I didn't mean to upset you."

"You didn't. It happened almost 600 years ago."

"How old are you, anyway?"

"I happen to be 1000. How old are you?"

"I am 1200 years old. I died by choice. I had spotted a vampire and was interested. I asked the vampire if he would change me, he said yes, and ever since then I have been happy."

"I married Edmond, and he gave me the choice of becoming a vampire or losing him forever."

"So you loved him very much."

"And still do. He was killed by a hunter at that very castle. I killed the hunter, and then moved. I also killed the hunter's son, who was just like his father. We don't kill for fun."

"Except tonight?"

"Tonight's different. Let's go dance around the body while we're talking about death. The dancing is the best part of our weddings. And then the burning."

We danced and watched the body burn. Everybody waved as the newly married vampire couple flew away to their love nest.

"John, one nice thing about the weddings is that the clothing has not changed over the centuries."

"And we should know."

We flew home together, laughing. The sun was going to rise soon. For the first time since Edmond died I felt I could be with someone again.

Edmond will always be my first love, but he is dead. I got on with my life when he died, but something always held me back. That night I let go of Edmond. After 600 years I could love again. I cried–but felt relieved.

The next night, after work, I started a new life with John.

CHAPTER 10

The blood says whatever needs to be said

John and I didn't spend much time apart. We eventually moved in together–he into my house.

He got along well with my children. He even got involved in the business.

I was in love, but not the same as I had felt for Edmond.

"John, I would like to talk to you."

"What about?"

"I am a woman of the twentieth century, and in these 1970s women are beginning to be more independent. It is okay to ask men out on dates, and even to ask them to marry you."

"Will you repeat that?"

"Certainly. I said it is okay for a woman to ask a man to marry her. The night I met you I said goodbye to Edmond. Forever. My love for him had held me back for six centuries. Sure, I cried the night he died, and after that. But I didn't really let go. Now I want to start a life with you. John?"

"Yes?"

"Will you marry me?"

"I will marry you. I love you."

I walked up and kissed him. We moved to the bed. He removed my dress. I took off his shirt and pants. Our white skin glowed in the darkness. He started caressing me with kisses. Our canine teeth came out.

I bit him on the neck and drank his sweet blood. When I withdrew my teeth, he bit me on the breast. It felt so good when he drank my blood!

He entered my body. This hadn't happened to me in 600 years. I bit into his chest. Such ecstasy!

We lay on the bed afterwards, just talking. When the sun rose we fell asleep.

The next night we planned dinner with the children. We wanted to tell them, or rather, John wanted to, and I said he could.

"I have been smitten by your mother. She has asked me to marry her. I have said yes."

"Mother, we are so happy for you!" said Annabelle. "We have all found love, and it was your turn."

"I think Edmond would be happy for me."

"He is, Mother. Wherever he is, he knows you're happy now," said Josephine.

"I think you're right," I said.

"Of course she's right!" Alexander added.

The next night we got in touch with Marsha and Earl, the owners of Vampire Hill. The wedding was planned for the next full moon. I hadn't been married vampire-style, and John had never been married before.

I was very nervous before the wedding.

"Mother, don't worry," Josephine said reassuringly. "I have been through it. It feels wonderful."

Annabelle came into the room. "It's time to get dressed."

Then Arthur walked in.

"Mother, I'm so happy for you!"

"Are you kids ready?" I asked.

In unison: "We're ready."

Full moon, clear sky, everybody wearing red. Victim was on the table, and we were all hungry. When the man saw us, he shook with fear. He tried to leave, but he was tied down by his mind.

Our sharp canine teeth came out. I could smell the fear in his blood. John and I bit into his neck together. I could feel his life drain very fast. When he died, we pulled out. John took my hand, and we started dancing around the table. The other vampires joined in, dancing until midnight.

At midnight we burned the body. Everybody gathered by the fire as John and I threw him in. Our union was complete. There aren't words in the vampire marriage ceremony. The blood says whatever needs to be said.

When we got home we burned our clothes, and then made love as husband and wife. My life was complete again.

John continued with me in the business, as did my children. Annabelle and Doug had finally decided on marriage, and had the ceremony as John and I had.

Josephine and Alexander had an addition to their family. They had found a tough girl on the streets, who had run away from her foster home. Josephine went home to change the air system in their house, in case the girl came to live with them.

"Kathy, how would you like to spend some time with us?" Alexander asked.

"What? I don't even know you!"

"Did you know your foster parents when they took you in?"

"No, I didn't."

"Well, I'm Alexander. The woman who was with me is Josephine, my wife."

"Why do you care about me? I'm worth nothing."

"You are worth something. You're a person, aren't you? We will contact the adoption agency to make it official. What do you say? Will you give it a try?"

Josephine came back. "What did she say?"

"She hasn't answered yet."

"So, you're Josephine," said Kathy, with her jet-black hair in a ponytail.

"Kathy. Is it all right if I call you Kathy?"

"Do what you want. I don't care."

"You should care. It's your own name."

"So what?"

"So what? It belongs to you. Tell you what, we have some other clothes and a warm bed."

"A warm bed sounds nice, but I like my clothes."

"But wouldn't you like some clean ones? I brought some."

"One night only."

"Funny, that's what my brother, sister, and I said when we met our parents. The parents that cared."

"What do you mean?"

"We met people who cared for us, and we stayed with them. Nice to be loved!"

"I don't know what that feels like."

"Alexander, this is awful!"

"Kathy?"

"Now what, Al?"

"My name is Alexander."

"Whatever suits you."

"Thank you. Will you please come home with us? For a little while?"

"I do want a place to stay. Okay."

When they arrived home there was food. After Kathy was done eating, they told her what not to do here.

"I've been wondering why it's so dark."

"We like the dark. That's one of the rules–no daylight. We sleep during the day."

"Why?"

"We're not going to answer that question right now. You will go to school, starting tomorrow."

"I will go to school. And I like you two. So: I will come back."

"But we must ask you to leave before daylight and come back after dark."

"Why, Josephine?"

"We can't answer that. Will you do it?"

"Yes. Why not? You are giving me a place to stay."

Josephine came to see me. I helped them find a woman to take Kathy after school and on weekends. When Josephine and Alexander finally explained their situation to Kathy, she understood, especially when they told her that she wouldn't even be able to breathe in the house during the day.

Years later Kathy graduated from high school. No longer a tough little girl. She was a beautiful woman, hair down to her waist, good grades, very athletic.

She loved our stories of when we were alive, and after we died. She realized she couldn't have gotten a better history lesson.

When she reached age twenty-one they offered her immortality, which she accepted. Josephine and Alexander felt their secret was safe because she knew that if she told it she would lose them.

Kathy had to choose whom she wanted to change her. She chose John, her "grandpa." Josephine and Alexander were not hurt by her decision. John looks and is about thirty-three–that is, his age when he died. He is the oldest in both ages in the current family.

John took Kathy to his bedroom.

"Kathy, are you ready to do this?"

"Yes, I am, John."

"This may hurt, but not much."

His teeth came out. She had never seen anyone feeding, so she had never seen the teeth. They shocked her.

"Will you do it now?"

"Do you want to be human one more day?"

"No. I am tired of being human. Your lifestyle fits me better."

"Okay. Here goes."

John bit into her neck. She gasped, but then got more comfortable. As he drank, she saw visions—the past; her parents' deaths; her life with her present family and all the failed foster homes too. Then she saw into the future, and how good her life would be.

Suddenly the visions stopped. John had withdrawn his teeth. He took a knife and cut his chest. She could smell the blood. She wanted it. She placed her mouth on the cut and sucked the blood like she would die without it.

"That is enough," John said. "It is time for you to sleep."

"But I want more."

"You will get more tomorrow night. You must let the process work itself out."

Kathy fell asleep. John covered her with a blanket and put the light seal on the window—not even moonlight could enter.

When John was back in the living room, Josephine asked, "Is it done?"

"Yes. It went very well. She wanted even more blood."

"That reminds me of some people!" I smirked. "Have you two chosen a victim for her?"

"We have yet to, Solena. We've been trying to find someone who won't be missed."

"It is harder in these times," I said, "but possible. Have you tried a homeless person?"

"Yes, we have looked there."

"Why don't I find one for you?" I offered.

"Mother, we have to. She's our daughter."

"I understand. That's why I had to find the first victims for the three of you."

Alexander and Josephine found a homeless person with no one around her. They brought her to the house, put her in one of the bedrooms that wasn't steel lined, and bolt locked her in. She knew she was going to die, and if the victim knows, it is harder to kill them, except when the occasion is a wedding.

When night came, Kathy woke up. She was very thirsty, and smelled blood. She walked into the living room.

"Good evening, Kathy."

"Good evening, Mother. And Father."

"How do you feel this evening?" Alexander asked. "I remember when I woke up for the first time I had no idea what was going on."

"Well, honey, you had fallen off the cliff," said Josephine, "and it was the only thing I could do to save you."

"I know. I was in shock, though. How would you feel if you woke up dead?"

"I did have a choice, and you didn't. But why are we talking about this now? Kathy, you must be hungry."

"I am."

"Then come with us."

They unlocked the bedroom door.

"What do I do, Mother?"

"You must kill her. This is the only victim you have to kill."

There was a mirror in the room. Kathy's appearance surprised her. But hunger was driving her crazy.

The girl shook with fear. Kathy's teeth had already come out. She licked the girl's salty neck, and then bit into it. The blood was even better than John's. She drank until the girl was dead.

Kathy looked in the mirror again. Her skin was an unnatural pink. Her jet-black hair stuck out. She liked the way she looked.

She and her parents took the body to Vampire Hill, where they burned it. She had heard so much about the Hill; now she got to see where her family went a lot.

Kathy enjoyed learning how to fly, and to use the rest of her powers. She hunted on her own, and still does.

She took over running the clothing store. I didn't want her involved in my other business.

Now it was the late 1980s. Trouble was brewing–trouble that would rock the New York vampire world. Trouble that I had to take care of, a bit of unfinished business.

CHAPTER 11

Do you believe the story?

Ever since he could remember, Willy Chemberlin had been interested in vampires. When he was a kid his father told him a story about his namesake many-greats-grandfather, William, who was killed by a vampire in 1391. Then that William's son was killed. Not many family members believed the story.

Willy, now twenty-five and with dark hair down to his shoulder, tied back, went to the bookstore.

"Well, Willy. I wondered when you were coming."

"Hi, Mr. Carter. I'm glad the books came in."

"I've always wondered why you're so interested in vampires."

"A fair question. A family story says I'm named after a man who was killed by a vampire, and whose son was too."

"An interesting story, but probably not true. What year did this happen?"

"1391. In England."

"And when was his son killed?"

"Thirty years later."

"Do you believe the story?"

"I don't know. But it prompted me to study vampires. I think they could exist."

"I've never met anybody so interested in them!"

Willy returned to his modest apartment in the Bronx. He couldn't afford much on his salary as a piano player at a night club.

It is 1991, the new year one week old. Willy was walking to work and saw someone strange. A man with deathly white skin. Willy had to warm up with the singer, so he hurried on.

"Willy, you're late."

"Sorry, boss. Hi, Brenda."

"Hi Willy. You're late."

"I know, I know. Something strange happened on the way here. I saw this man who was deathly pale. He looked dead."

"How could he be dead if he was walking?"

"I could think of something, but it couldn't be true."

"What are you talking about?"

"Vampires."

"Vampires? What do you mean?"

"The walking dead"

"I know what they are. Why would you believe they even exist?"

"I have reason to believe. I don't really care to explain right now. We have to warm up."

Brenda sang several sets, then, when she was on a break, the man Willy saw earlier walked in.

"Brenda."

"What is it, Willy?"

"The man I saw tonight is here. He is at the far right table."

"He doesn't look pale."

"I know. That confuses me. I wonder where his color came from."

"Stop staring at him, Willy. It's not polite."

"Get back to work, you two!"

"Sorry, boss. Willy, don't look over there anymore."

After the last set was over, Willy left. The man left at the same time. Willy followed him and stayed on his trail all night.

Just before sunrise the man walked into his house, with its windows painted black. Willy tried to open the door, but the man had locked it. Willy placed a slip of paper in a crack on the outside of the door.

Willy went home and got some sleep. He made sure to wake up before the sun set. He went to the strange man's house and noticed the slip of paper was still there. He hid in a corner.

When the sun was fully set, the man left the house–deathly white again. He went into an alley, where there was a homeless person. Willy saw the two talking, the strange man looking around as if to see whether there was anyone else there. The homeless man followed the strange man into an empty building, and Willy followed, out of sight but where he could see what happened. He was hoping something would happen soon, since he was about to be late for work.

The strange man bit into the homeless man's neck and drank. Then he ran out of the building. He almost saw Willy.

Willy ran to the homeless man to see if he was alive. To Willy's amazement, he was. Willy helped him up, then ran to work, making it just in time.

When he told Brenda what happened, she didn't believe him. He knew what he saw. He didn't know why the man didn't die. Every book he had read said that vampires kill every time they feed, or at least slowly over time. The victims eventually die.

He kept tabs on the homeless man. He just kept getting better.

Willy had heard about a woman who had dealt with vampires before. Everybody said she was crazy. But he went to Dr. Mary Wilson's office and asked her why the vampire didn't kill the man.

"After years of research into vampires, I have found out they don't kill when they feed."

Willy told her the story of his forefathers.

"Willy, I have interviewed vampires. They are not bad creatures. They are trying to exist, just like us. The reason a vampire killed your relative is because a loved one of hers was probably killed by him."

"You're on her side?"

"What would you do if a family member of yours was killed? As a human, you would want revenge. Vampires are still part human inside. They still have feelings, they still care."

"How can they? They are no longer human!"

"As I just said. They still care. Vampires have to live with humans in this world. They have to get along with us, or they will be in danger of not existing."

"I still don't understand how you can be on their side."

"Who says I am? I'm just saying I understand them, and that I don't think they're as bad as people think they are. Talking to vampires, I have gotten their point of view."

"I think they are bad. They should be destroyed."

"I can't stop you. But I may try. Some vampires are my friends now. And if you try to follow me, I'm sure you will be in danger from my friends. Just like I protect them, they protect me."

"You are protecting them? How dare you!"

"Please leave now. I don't like your tone of voice."

Willy left. The sun was going to set in a little while. When it did, Mary Wilson made a phone call.

"Hello. By the Light of the Moon Escort Service. We always do the best we can to serve you."

"This is Mary Wilson. I would like to speak to Solena Wilshire, please."

"She is busy right now. May she call you back"

"Yes. This is urgent. Have her call me as soon as she can. She knows my number. Thanks."

I came back after I was done with a client.

"Solena, there is a very important message for you."

"Who is it from?"

"Mary Wilson. And it's urgent."

I called her up.

"Mary, this is Solena. What's up?"

"I can't tell you over the phone. Can we meet?"

"What do you have in mind?"

"I don't want to put you in danger."

"Danger? What are you talking about?"

"I said, I can't explain it here. Let's meet at my house. You may want to enter through the back door, and don't bring a car."

"I could fly."

"It's the safest way. I don't want you to be spotted."

"Okay. But first I have to call my husband to tell him I won't be home right away." I tried to explain to John, but it was difficult when I didn't even know what the urgency was.

"Solena, I'm so glad you're here. Did anyone see you?"

"No, I made sure I wasn't seen. That's hard to do when flying, but possible. Now, why did you call me here?"

"Do you remember when I was searching for vampires to interview, and I found you?"

"Yes. And I would never have talked to you if you hadn't seemed trustworthy."

"The minute I saw you I knew you wouldn't hurt me. And now I don't want you hurt."

"I can't really be hurt."

"The better word is 'killed.' You are my friend. And I care about you."

"What is your point?"

"A man came by here today. He had seen a vampire feed. I could tell he knows a lot about your kind. He thinks you are inherently evil. I know different. He knows about you personally, also. Well sort of. You killed one of his grandfathers. In 1391. And then thirty years later ..."

"Would he happen to be a Chemberlin?"

"He gave me his first name, Willy, but didn't add his last name. I think he is going to kill that vampire he saw. Willy knows a lot."

"I knew this would start up again some day. This is why we moved to America, so we could keep an eye on the family. I just wish I knew which Chemberlin it is. I would like to take care of him right away, but that won't be possible."

"Do you mean kill him?"

"I will have to. Otherwise no vampires will be safe. Please don't try to stop me."

"That is why I called you. I think both races can survive in this world, but in order for that to happen, some sacrifices have to occur. In fact, I warned him not to do anything, or he would be sorry. Friends help out friends."

"I'm glad you called me. I will find out soon enough if this vampire dies."

"Now what are you talking about?"

"I can't tell you. It's information for vampires only. And there are no exceptions to this rule, or else all vampires will be threatened."

"I won't ask any more questions."

"I should leave now. I have work to do. Thank you. You have saved many vampires from certain death."

Willy knew the vampire's patterns, especially that he came home right before sunrise. If Willy barricaded the door, the vampire wouldn't have enough time to get inside.

Willy barred the door with crosses, and blocked every entrance. He even did the same with surrounding buildings.

The vampire ran, reached the door, and stopped. He could feel the sun burning him. He saw Willy laughing at him. He cursed Willy. He saw crosses all over, and realized there was no hope.

The vampire went down with dignity. He stood still and let it happen. When the sun was fully risen, he was dead. There was nothing left.

Willy walked away happy. He had a new hobby.

The next night, up on Vampire Hill, a vampire was missing. Everybody wondered where Tim was. His best friend was getting married that night. I was at the wedding.

Tony and I went to Tim's home, and found crosses. We knew he was dead. And I knew who committed the murder. Tony and I both vowed revenge. I knew deaths would continue if I didn't stop Willy.

I needed help. Willy knew how to deal with vampires, and he probably had a strong mind, just like his grandfathers. I needed to do my task quickly.

Before anyone else died.

CHAPTER 12

I have to face him

After Tony and I found Tim's house surrounded by crosses, we went back to Vampire Hill. Everyone was shocked, and knew something had to be done. This was more important than a wedding. We put out the word to every vampire we could reach.

The next night all the vampires who had been contacted met at Vampire Hill–members and nonmembers (the membership rules were tossed for the night, indeed for the whole crisis).

We knew Willy couldn't totally wipe us out. But he could lower our number, and it was getting dangerous to make new vampires– because of the bodies. They can't all be disposed of at Vampire Hill. Cops would get suspicious of the smell.

Most thought it wouldn't take too long to get Willy. I knew different. I knew his forefathers. And it had taken spotting only one vampire to persuade Willy that the stories were true.

I was worried for the first time in hundreds of years. I knew that I had to kill Willy; otherwise, I was going to die.

I went to see Dr. Wilson the next night. I told her about the vampires meeting. She was interested, but knew not to ask too many questions.

We looked up Willy's address in the phone book. Mary understood that I had to catch him off guard.

We went to his apartment, in a dingy building. He clearly didn't have much money, and maybe couldn't afford to run. A knock on the door got no response.

I forced the door open with my superhuman strength. The apartment was sparsely furnished: TV, couch, kitchen table, end table, and the bedroom didn't have much either: just a bed and a dresser. The bathroom was off the bedroom, the bathtub in the kitchen.

We waited. Willy came home about one in the morning. Willy was curious that the door was already open. I was hiding.

"Dr. Wilson, what are you doing here? And how did you get in?"

"I opened the door," I said.

Willy looked at me, scared.

"What, who? It's you! I know you. You have been described by every son in every generation. You are the vampire that killed my ancestors. I want you dead."

"Too bad. I'm already dead. I've been dead for a thousand years."

Willy knew he had to do something. He just didn't know what.

"Willy, I want you to leave us alone. We don't mean to hurt humans. We just want to get along with you. Mary knows this."

"But you're evil! You kill people!"

"I have read of–and even met–people more evil than vampires will ever be."

"But Satan made you."

"No, Satan didn't make me. My husband made me. He happens to be really dead. Thanks to your family, I lost the man I loved."

Willy had no response. He was seeing some human in me, in this vampire, but he figured it wasn't possible, because he had been taught that vampires can't be human.

"Yes we can, Willy. That part that is alive is human. Our soul doesn't die. We still feel. We still care."

"I hate you," said Willy.

I grabbed him and lifted him in the air. He was shaking.

"Willy, leave us alone. We don't want to hurt you. But you force us to."

Suddenly, Willy remembered he was wearing a cross around his neck. He grabbed it and put it toward my face. I turned, and was forced to drop him.

Willy ran out of the apartment. Mary and I ran after him. I sped past him, while baring my fangs.

He turned back, and bumped into Mary. She held him tight. I walked towards him. He wormed out of Mary's grasp and ran as fast as he could.

I didn't know why Mary hadn't grabbed his cross. I didn't dare go after him now; he might follow me. I flew home.

I called Kim, my assistant/secretary.

"Hello."

"Kim, did I wake you?"

"No."

"Of course I did. I'm sorry, but this is important."

"I know you wouldn't call me this early if it wasn't. Okay, what's wrong?"

"I need you to run the business for a while."

"I do anyway, during the day."

"I mean at night, too. You know what I am. And I trust you. Something from my past is haunting me. I am in danger of losing my life."

"What?"

"I will explain later. You have to run the business. I can't come in until this crisis is over."

"Okay, I trust you."

"Get some sleep. You're going to have long days–and nights. Don't open the office until noon. Isn't business pretty slow until then, anyway?"

"Yes, it's slow in the morning."

"You know which employees serve which clients?"

"Yes, I do."

"I will fax a memo. Good night–or, Good morning."

I called my family. They came over.

"Solena, I don't want to lose you," said John.

"You won't. But I have to face him. Sometime. Or I will never be safe."

"I know," John replied. "The rest of the family is here; we can talk about this later."

"I am done talking about this. I have no choice in the matter."

"Mom, what's up?"

"Annabelle, I didn't reveal this information at the vampire meeting. The man whose ancestor Edmond killed wants to kill me."

"What?" gasped Annabelle.

"It's what I said. We are not going to be working at the escort service during this crisis. Kim will run the office. We are going to hunt very carefully. And Kathy, I'm going to shut down the clothing store for a while."

"Please don't!"

"I have to, Kathy. I want you safe too. The business will stay afloat; I have enough money."

"I understand. I just wish you didn't have to do that. I really enjoy working in the store."

"This isn't forever. I'm going to get this guy."

"I know you will, Gram. I know you will!"

Willy went out every night in search of vampires. After a couple of weeks he spotted one. A vampire named Helle had just arrived from Denmark and had taken over a warehouse. Though she had heard there were lots of vampires in New York, she hadn't found any. She was planning to meet her friend Britta.

Britta told her how dangerous it was for vampires, and persuaded Helle to come stay with her. But Helle had to get her bag first. It was getting close to sunrise, so Helle decided to stay one more night at the warehouse. When she got back to it, the sun was rising, and there were crosses all over the building.

She couldn't run. She was burning up. The flames overtook her body. In agonizing pain, she died.

Britta woke up the next night, expecting Helle to arrive soon. Helle had told her, telepathically, where she was staying, so Britta knew where to go looking for her.

She found the crosses; luckily there was a door where there wasn't a cross. No Helle. Britta knew she was dead.

Britta went home and cried, then to Vampire Hill, where she told us.

I really had to get him now.

CHAPTER 13

Like it was yesterday

"I have been having that feeling again, Richard."

"What feeling?"

"The feeling that she is going to die."

"Edmond, Solena is not going to die."

"I'm not sure about that. I've lost her, but I don't want her to die."

"You lost her because you were afraid of what she would think. I should have sent you back when you woke up. But I wanted to get to know you. You are my vampire son."

"Well, thank you. I've always wanted to know my father. But someone I love is in trouble. I have to go to her."

"She has met someone else already."

"I know. I cried when in a vision I saw the two of them together in New York. But I have to go back to her. I also miss my children. Do you want to come with me?"

"I would like to. I want to see her reaction, and to see if you are right about her being in danger."

They fed, then flew out of England. Edmond hoped he wasn't too late, but if he had to lose Solena as a wife, he still wanted to be her friend. He knew, too, that he had a grandchild. He wanted to get to know her, and his children's spouses.

Partway through the second night they landed in New York. (You may wonder where they slept during the daylight hours of their Atlantic crossing–we fly fast but are no match for jet planes. They stayed with vampire friends in Nuuk, Greenland. Also, flying west, against the earth's rotation, is advantageous, since darkness is extended. And it was January, when nights in the northern hemisphere are longer anyway.)

They went to Josephine and Alexander's home. Edmond knocked, and Kathy answered the door. She knew that the man who was killing vampires didn't knock.

"Hello."

"Hello. Are you perhaps Kathy?"

"How do you know my name?"

"I can explain that later. Is your mother at home?"

"I will get her."

"Well, Edmond, here goes."

"I'm excited, Father. You're about to meet your granddaughter!"

Josephine came to the door. Alexander was with her. Kathy told them a strange man was waiting.

"Yes, what, Father?! It can't be you. You died 600 years ago!"

"Josephine, I have missed you so much!"

Edmond embraced his daughter. At first she didn't return the hug, she was so shocked.

"Please come in, sir," said Alexander.

"Edmond, please. This is Richard, my father."

"You found him."

"No, Josephine, he found me."

"Alexander is right–please come in."

"I see you have the same system we had at the castle."

"Mom made sure of that."

"How is she?"

"I will have to tell you about that later. This is your grand-daughter, Kathy."

"I know. I have kept tabs on all of you. I was scared of what Solena would say. I will explain later."

"Josephine, I have heard a lot about you," said Richard. "Your father loves you all, and wanted to come back, but he was really scared. Come here and give me a hug."

"Grandpa! How nice to meet you. Father talked about you, but we didn't know who you were."

Tears all around.

Josephine called her sister and brother and asked them to come over the next night. Then she called her mother and asked the same.

"Why do I have to wait?" Edmond asked.

"Because it is dangerous with that man out there. I don't want them hurt."

"Do you mean Willy Chemberlin?"

"Yes. How do you know?"

"That is the main reason I came back now. Your mother is in danger of dying."

"She knows that."

"I have the feeling that she'll die if something isn't done fast. I know where Willy is. He has to be taken care of. This is my fault."

"No, it isn't, Dad. She also helped kill his son. Do you remember Christina?"

"Yes."

"When we were living in Greece she came to visit us. His son was killing English vampires at an alarming rate, before they could leave, and at that time there weren't many English vampires at all. I met Alexander in Greece."

"I haven't said how honored I am to meet you," said Alexander. "They got to Greece just after you were attacked. I met Josephine when they arrived. It didn't take long to fall in love with her."

"That's not hard to believe! Josephine's a wonderful person, and vampire."

"You're embarrassing me, Dad. You two will stay here. We have extra beds."

"You sleep in beds? We don't, in England."

"We have light-proof rooms; modern technology, you know. We are quite safe. There are two extra bedrooms."

"How do you survive? What about money?"

"Mom owns a clothing store, and gives the profits to us. She has another business, from which she keeps the profit. We invest the money she gives us, and it's doing well."

"Very smart. Are your brother and sister doing this too?"

"Yes. We can't really find a job. People would suspect. Kathy?"

"Yes."

"How old were you when you died?"

"I was twenty-one. I died in the early 1980s. They found me when I was ten. I was really tough then. I ran away from a foster home–just one of many. They gave me a better life, and I love them very much."

"It shows. You're lucky. I am tired. Aren't you, Father?"

"Yes. It was a long flight."

"Dad, you know Mom has remarried," said Josephine.

"Yes. And I still love her the way I did when we first met."

It didn't take them long to fall asleep in their beds.

The next night Arthur and Jessica arrived first, then Annabelle and Doug. Solena called and said she and John were going to be a little late.

Dad came out of his room. "Arthur, Annabelle, how are you?"

"Father!" they said at the same time. In shock, Doug and Jessica had trouble understanding what was going on.

"Annabelle, how can this be your father? He is dead," Doug blurted out.

"I'm not dead. My name is Edmond."

"I'm Doug."

"And you are?"

"Jessica."

"What a beautiful name! And this is their grandfather, Richard."

"Hello. I've been very eager to meet all of you."

"This is your father, Dad? You didn't know who he was."

"I know, Arthur. He found me."

Even more tears and hugs.

Then, a knock at the door.

"That must be Mom," said Josephine.

"Will you let me get the door?"

"If you want, Dad."

When Solena saw Edmond, she was speechless.

"Solena, I have missed you so much!"

"Ah."

"It's me. I know it's hard to believe."

"Ah, Edmond."

"I know this is a shock."

"A shock? You died."

"I almost died."

"I am so happy you survived."

Solena hugged and kissed him. John watched nervously.

"Solena, I would appreciate it if you didn't do that."

"I understand, Solena. He is your husband."

"Yes he is, Edmond. John, this was a very big surprise. Edmond, where have you been?"

"I have been in England. Come in. I will tell you all. You four know what happened until you went into the castle."

"But the rest of the story was never told, Edmond."

"I will now tell that part, Solena. We were followed by one of Willy's forefathers. It was near sunrise. We were out late that night."

"I remember it like it was yesterday."

"So do I, Solena. I told all of you to go into the castle. There was no time left. The man and I started fighting. I was getting weaker. But I used my last burst of energy to knock the man out. The sun was almost fully in the sky. I imagine you heard my screams. I was burning. I got into one of the secret compartments on the outside of the castle.

"You four–Annabelle, Josephine, Arthur, and Solena–could probably feel me dying. But when we go to sleep, as you know, we stop feeling. So, most likely you all thought I was dead.

"I slowly woke. Richard had sensed that I was waking. He came to me, and when I awoke, I was healed. This was almost a hundred years later. Richard told me the year. He explained that he had made me a vampire. I wanted to come back to you, but I also wanted to get to know the man who made me what I am. And he wanted to get to know me."

"I am very glad I came to get him. But I think he stayed too long. He lost you, Solena."

"I realized I had to get on with my life, thinking Edmond was dead. Edmond, I still love you. John knows that."

"I do know and understand that," said John. "She has told me all about you. But I love her so much."

"I know that, John. I want to compete for her, but she has to decide. And I think she has made her choice."

"You are right. I have made my choice. I don't want to hurt you, Edmond, but I love John and am going to stay with him."

"Solena, I was afraid of how you would react to my coming back. I blew my chance. But I came back to warn you. I had a feeling that you would die. I knew I had to come. I know where Willy is."

"How can you? I have been trying to find out, but without success."

"He fell asleep at night, which he hadn't before. That was stupid. This will be his downfall."

"Let's get to work. Edmond, I have someone I'd like you to meet. We will go there now. She will help us."

CHAPTER 14

It doesn't look too good

We went to see Dr. Wilson.

"Solena, she's human!" Edmond blurted.

"Yes, I know. We can trust her. She informed me about Willy. ... Oh! Dr. Wilson, this is my first love, Edmond."

"Edmond? I thought you said he was dead."

"That's what we all thought. He came here last night. He is going to help us. And this is Richard, his father."

"Pleased to meet you both. Do you have an idea?"

"I know where Willy is staying. And while we were flying here, Richard told me about Vampire Court. I'd never experienced it, or even heard about it."

"Richard, what do you mean by Vampire Court?" I asked.

"Willy will be captured. I know a judge who is good; she has run other trials. It's like a human court of law, but the defendant will become a vampire in the end. The jury has to decide whether he is to die the way he has killed vampires.

"But you have to help us capture him, Dr. Wilson. He will get a fair trial. The jury vampires won't be from this venue–and I know which vampires to get.

"Since Willy wears a cross, he will have to be stunned so you can take his cross off. Then we'll take him to where the trial can begin."

I went to Vampire Hill. The building had the necessary rooms–for incarceration and for judgment.

The next night we went back to Dr. Wilson's. She had gotten the stun gun.

We went to where Willy was staying, a place even cheaper than his apartment. I forced the door open, with the knob only.

He was sleeping. Mary stunned him with the gun. She grabbed his cross and put it in her purse.

I picked Willy up, and we flew to Vampire Hill. He was chained, then locked in the cell. When he woke up, he had no idea where he was.

Someone entered the room. "My name is Brad. I am your counsel. You are on trial for crimes against vampires."

Willy reached in his shirt for his cross–and came up empty.

"The cross is gone. I flew in yesterday, to help you. Though I can't believe it, because I am what you are trying to kill."

"What is going on?"

"You are on trial for murdering two vampires. This is Vampire Court. You will become a vampire during the proceeding, but your fate still won't be clear."

Brad sat down on a chair. A light had been turned on already.

"I think you can tell I don't want to do this, but I have done it before."

"Stay away from me and leave me alone!"

"If you don't let me help you, you will surely die. I mean really die. These vampires want you dead, and I don't know if I disagree with them."

"I thought you were supposed to help me."

"And I will. You have the right to a defense. That is all I can guarantee."

"Will there be a jury?"

"Yes, of vampires from different parts of the country. The judge and the prosecutor will be from elsewhere, too. So it is as fair as it can be."

"When is this going to happen?"

"In a couple of days. Your family has been contacted and told that you have left town. They won't worry, believe me. Nobody human knows where you are."

"Where am I?"

"I can tell you, because you will die here in one way for sure. You are at Vampire Hill. These chains are tough even for vampires to break, by the way. Why do you want to kill us? I'm not talking about one vampire. That won't be brought up at the trial."

"Why not?"

"Because of what I've been told."

"I think you are inherently evil. You kill people!"

"You can think that, but it will be your downfall, since you will be joining us. It doesn't look too good. I can almost guess what is going to happen.

"I have to go prepare your defense. Some food will be brought to you."

The judge arrived.

"Richard! It is good to see you again."

"Hello, Shari. I'm glad you agreed to come. Was it a long flight?"

"Not really. You did contact me the night before. I left soon after I woke up."

"How is it in the state of Minnesota?"

"A bit chilly. It's winter."

"I should visit you sometime."

"That would be nice. Has a jury been selected yet?"

"They are flying in tonight. Your friend Susan, the prosecutor, is coming from France for the trial. This has not happened in a long time."

"Why are we having a trial?"

"The defendant is Willy Chemberlin."

"I know that last name."

"You should. That family did a lot of vampire killing in England."

"Didn't a vampire take care of them?"

"Yes, but their descendants kept coming back."

"I have no doubt that he will die, then. What does he believe in?"

"That all vampires are inherently evil."

"That is just not true. You know personally."

"I may have to bring it up, but I don't care to. It's information that not every vampire is privy to. I have some things to do. I'll see you when the trial starts. Good luck!"

"Thanks. I am going to enjoy this. I haven't judged a trial in a long time."

CHAPTER 15

An ancient spell

The trial was about to begin.

"Brad, what do you think is going to happen?" Willy asked, nervously.

"I don't know. Cases have been won and lost by humans. What you have to show is that you are truly sorry, and are worthy of being a vampire. I have to tell you the truth: I don't think you are. The prosecutor has to prove that you killed the vampires. This is easy to do. I can even tell by looking at you that you are guilty of the murders. And we don't look kindly on people who kill us. Just like you don't look kindly on us.

"One claim you make is that we don't feel anymore. We don't like that charge against us, and it becomes part of our case against you."

"But you can't feel. You're dead!"

"I have a wife. I could be with her right now, but I have to be here, with you. We do love."

"You can't. I won't believe that."

"Then you will die for real. I might as well leave, then. You don't want my help."

"I want to live."

"If the verdict goes in your favor, you will still die. You will be a vampire. You will get our point of view."

"I don't want your point of view. I want out of here!"

"That is not going to happen."

They were told the trial was about to start.

"This is going to be hard. I will do my best."

Willy looked, and saw all the vampires. He didn't want to be one of them.

The judge entered the room.

"Please be seated, fellow vampires," said Shari. "I am honored to be the judge at this trial. I am going to make sure the trial is fair. Prosecution, please make your opening statement."

"Thank you, Your Honor. Vampires of the jury, I am going to prove that William Chemberlin killed two vampires without a valid claim of defending himself. He killed them out of anger at all of us, wanting to destroy all of our kind. He believes we are inherently evil, and that we can't feel. He shows us no compassion. He has fallen into the thinking of almost every human."

"Thank you. Public Defender, please present your opening statement."

Brad stood up. "Thank you, Your Honor. I am going to prove that William Chemberlin is sorry for believing that vampires are evil. For thinking we don't feel. Thank you for listening to me, distinguished vampire jury."

"Ms. Prosecutor, you may call your first witness."

"Thank you. I call Solena Wilshire."

I came up.

"Solena, do you swear to tell the truth and nothing but the truth?" asked the bailiff.

"Yes, I do."

The Prosecutor got up from the chair.

"Solena, what do you recall from the confrontation you had with William Chemberlin?"

"I remember going to his apartment with Dr. Mary Wilson. I opened the door, and we waited for him. When he came home, he was surprised to see Dr. Wilson. And when he saw me, he was shocked. He knew I was a vampire. He knew me.

"I have had bad relations with his ancestors. Dr Wilson and I talked to him. He wouldn't listen to us. He said we are all evil. I told him we want to get along with humans, but he didn't believe me. He said we can't feel because we aren't human anymore. After that, I picked him up, but he pulled out a cross he was wearing around his neck, and I had to let him go."

"Is that cross anywhere around here?"

"Dr. Wilson has it. She took it when we detained him."

"Please continue with the rest of your story."

"There isn't much else, except he said vampires come from Satan. I told him I come from Edmond. Soon after that he ran away. We lost him."

"How did you detain him?"

"Edmond was supposedly killed by one of William Chemberlin's ancestors. But Edmond came back about a week ago–to the surprise of all of us. Edmond knew where Chemberlin was staying. He, Dr. Wilson, and I went there. Dr. Wilson numbed him with a stun gun. Then we brought him here."

"Thank you. Mr. Public Defender, you may question the witness now."

"Thank you, Your Honor. Solena, do you think William was serious about what he said?"

"Yes, I do. He seemed determined."

"Do you think he could change his mind about us?"

"No, I don't. It has been his family's past. I don't think there is anything that could change his mind."

"What did you do after you thought Edmond died?"

"I killed the man who killed him—or who I believed had killed him. I was very angry. He had killed other vampires also. Nothing was done about it. I wanted revenge for all the vampires that died by his hand."

"Isn't that what William was doing? Getting revenge for all his forefathers' deaths?"

"I don't know. I can't go into his mind. He had closed it off."

"Thank you. That is all."

"You may step down now, Ms. Wilshire."

"Thank you, Your Honor."

"Brad, why did you bring up the past?" the defendant asked the defender in a whisper.

"Because, Willy," the defender whispered back, "I thought it your best chance. It casts a shadow on Solena Wilshire. We need that shadow of doubt, or you have no hope."

"Ms. Prosecutor, you may call your next witness."

"Thank you, Your Honor. I would like to call Richard Cantebarry."

Richard walked up to the witness stand.

"Richard, do you swear to tell the whole truth and nothing but the truth?" the bailiff asked.

"I do."

"Richard, how do you know the Chemberlin family?"

"I know about all of the family, because of Edmond Chilstrom and Solena Wilshire."

"And how do you know Edmond Chilstrom and Solena Wilshire?"

"I am Edmond's father."

The jury looked surprised.

"Please continue, Mr. Cantebarry."

"As I said, I am Edmond's father. And Solena was his wife. I just met Solena this week."

"And what were the circumstances that brought you two here?"

"Edmond felt she was in danger."

"From whom"

"From William Chemberlin."

"What kind of danger did Edmond feel she was in?"

"He felt William Chemberlin would kill her."

"Do you think William Chemberlin is guilty of killing the two other vampires?"

Brad stood up. "I object, Your Honor. This would be hearsay. The witness has no idea whether my client is guilty or not."

"Sustained," said Shari.

"Sorry, Your Honor. I will drop the question. Richard, do you think Solena was in danger?"

"Yes, I do. After Edmond told me what happened 600 years ago. If I were William, I would want revenge too."

"William also believes vampires are inherently evil. Do you think this is true? Do you believe we come from Satan?"

"I know for a fact that we didn't."

"What do you mean?"

"I was made by the first vampire. This was when she was already over a thousand years old and was going a bit crazy."

"How did she become a vampire?"

"The question you should really be asking is this: How did we come about?

"There were a brother and sister, descended from Spanish people who came to England. They were witches–white witches. Their mother had died. The sister, Mary, knew of a spell that brings people back to life. But the spell could only be performed once.

"Mary thought she would try it. She couldn't be sure it would work, because she didn't know whether it had ever been used before.

"Mary was on her way on horseback to her mother's grave. She hit her head on a rock after being thrown when the horse was spooked by a snake. Her brother, Thomas, was worried about her, and was himself on the way to their mother's grave when he saw her. She died a few days later.

"Thomas was distraught. He had lost his whole family (his father had died years ago). He knew of the spell his sister had planned to use. A couple of weeks later he tried it on Mary, when, as he knew were the required conditions, the night was clear and the moon full.

"He arrived at his sister's grave, and with a torch lit ten candles, which he placed around the grave. He put the burning torch itself at the foot of the grave. He was wearing a red robe. He stood at the head of the grave and chanted this incantation: 'Fire and wood, day and night, with the strength of the moon, grant this woman back her life.'

"He took a knife and cut his hand. Blood dripped on the grave. He repeated the incantation, louder. All of a sudden, smoke started rising from the grave. He reiterated the incantation even louder a third time. When the smoke cleared, Mary was standing on top of the grave.

"Mary told me this story, with her brother by her side. The pressures of living reborn got to be too much for Mary. She eventually died by suicide, throwing herself into a fire. Thomas is still living, but I fear he may end up doing the same.

"Mary lived for two thousand years. She was not evil. Thomas is still alive. He is not evil. We came about from an ancient spell that could only work if love was present. The brother cared, didn't hate. They didn't worship Satan."

"Thank you, Richard. That is all."

Susan sat down.

"Does the Public Defender have any questions?"

"No, I don't, Your Honor."

"Prosecutor, you may call your next witness."

"Thank you. I call Edmond Chilstrom."

The bailiff swore him in.

"Mr. Chilstrom, do you confirm what Mr. Cantebarry said about Solena being in danger?"

"Yes, I do. I did feel that Solena was in danger."

"Was Solena telling the truth?"

"Yes, she was, as far as I know what happened 600 years ago. As for what happened this last month, I was reading her mind, so I can also confirm that information."

"Thank you. I have no more questions."

Mr. Public Defender, do you have any questions for this witness?"

"No, Your Honor, I don't."

"Mr. Chilstrom, you may stand down now."

Again, whispers between defendant and defender: "Brad, what are you doing?"

"Willy, these two witnesses are indistinguishable. I am going to put you on the stand."

"Why?"

"That is the only way possible to keep you alive."

"Ms. Prosecutor, do you have any other witnesses?"

"No, but I reserve the right to call up another witness at another time."

"Recognized. Mr. Public Defender, you may call your first witness."

"Thank you, Your Honor. I call William Chemberlin."

Willy walked up to the stand, and swore to tell the truth, the whole truth–but in a way that brought a foul look from the vampires: "Swearing to God, I do."

"William, did you kill those two vampires?"

"Yes, I did."

"Do you feel sorry for what you did?"

"I am starting to. I am starting to see another side of vampire."

"Do you still believe we are inherently evil?"

"No, I don't. Not after hearing the story Richard Cantebarry told."

"Thank you. That is all."

"Ms. Prosecutor, any questions for this witness?"

"No, I don't at this time. But I would like to recall him after the first part of the sentence is pronounced."

"Please step up the bench, both of you."

Brad and Susan approached the judge's bench.

"Susan, what are you up to?"

"I want to see how he really feels about being a vampire. He doesn't know what it's like, because he isn't one."

"Brad, do you agree to this?"

"Yes, I do. I would also like to know how he feels."

"You two may sit down now. William Chemberlin, will you please stand up?"

Willy stood up.

"William Chemberlin, I am going to pass the first part of your sentence. In a few days, I will hand down the rest of it. The jury will not decide until they have heard your additional testimony, if needed.

"The court is adjourned until two days hence. Brad, please transform him now."

Back in Willy's cell, he asked, "Brad, what are you going to do?"

"I am going to drink your blood, then you are going to drink mine."

"No, I am not."

"Yes, you will. You will have so much thirst. Now, sit down."

Brad bit into Willy's neck. Willy didn't like it. It hurt him. Brad stopped drinking. Willy was really thirsty. Brad cut his arm with a knife, and held it up to Willy.

Willy protested at first, but the blood looked good. He grabbed Brad's arm and gulped. Brad had to push him away. Brad picked Willy up and put him in a coffin that had been placed in the room. He closed the lid, then walked out.

"Brad, how did it go?" asked Judge Shari.

She had taken off her robe. Her long, slim body was visible now. Brad had put on more comfortable clothes.

"It went well. At first he didn't want to take my blood, but thirst overwhelmed him. I think he will kill easily tomorrow night. That is going to kill him. We don't like vampires to kill every night. But who knows?"

"You may be right, Brad. Let's go outside for a while. The sun is going to be rising soon. The other vampires have left. It is nice to be here when it's empty."

They went in later. They wondered how Willy would react. Every vampire wondered this. They wanted him to die, but it was up to the jury. Vampires in New York were restless.

CHAPTER 16

A single tear

Willy woke up. He felt strange. He was very hungry.

He got out of the coffin. He tried the door. It was locked. He found he was strong, but he still couldn't open it. Then he heard the door being unlocked. It was Brad.

"Why couldn't I open the door?"

"It was made so that even vampires couldn't break it down. This is a prison cell for vampires. You will feed now."

"No, I won't."

"Yes, you will. I know you are very thirsty. I was when I became one. You will act the same way you did last night. The thirst overwhelmed you.

"Bring in the victim now."

A scared homeless person walked in.

"You will take him, Willy."

Brad pushed Willy toward this man. Willy could smell him, his blood. He grabbed the man, his teeth came out, and he bit into his neck. Willy liked the taste of his blood; it felt good to kill him. He didn't like feeling like this, but he did.

The man dropped from his grasp. Brad took the man, and locked the door when he left, but not before telling Willy to figure out how he felt.

Brad came back an hour before sunrise. "Willy, how do you feel?"

"I feel good."

"Tell me the truth. How do you feel about killing?"

"I am not going to tell you. I figure I will be back on the stand. I understand I am in charge of my destiny. I have been sitting in this room and discovering new things about myself. Things about being a vampire.

"I just wish I could go outside. I am excited about discovering other things. This is all I'm going to say."

"If that's what you want. You should get into the coffin."

Willy got it, and Brad closed the lid.

Brad was unsure about what was going to happen. He figured he wouldn't ask any questions when Willy was on the stand. He was going to let Willy decide whether to hang himself or live forever–whether the arc of his story would be born by blood, died by blood, or died by blood, born by blood.

Brad went to bed, just wondering: What's next?

The following night another victim was placed in Willy's room. Willy killed the man, though he knew he didn't have to.

"I now call this trial to order," said Judge Shari. "Ms. Prosecutor, you said you wanted to question William Chemberlin. Please begin."

"Thank you, Your Honor. I call William Chemberlin.

"Willy, you know you were sworn in the other day. I must caution you to remember that. Because we will know."

Susan looked into his eyes and told him to tell the truth. He didn't expect this.

"Willy, what do you think about vampires?"

"I like being one. I just wish I could have encountered more victims yesterday. I enjoy killing."

"We have proof of that. I call into evidence the dead body from your feeding tonight."

"The evidence is recognized, Prosecutor. William, you may continue."

"I like the power. I am glad I'm a vampire."

"Thank you, William. That is all."

"Mr. Public Defender, do you have any questions?"

"No."

"William, you may stand down."

"Thank you, Your Honor."

"Are there any other witnesses?"

"No, Your Honor," said Brad and Susan.

"You may now present your closing arguments."

Susan got up.

"Thank you, Your Honor. Jury, I think I have proven that William Chemberlin is guilty of the lack of remorse. He has demonstrated that he likes to kill, and we don't. We want to get along with humans. I think William Chemberlin should be executed. Thank you."

"Mr. Public Defender, you may now present your closing statement."

"Thank you, Your Honor. Jury, I understand why the defendant would want to kill us. William Chemberlin is new to being a vampire. He doesn't understand our lifestyle. All he had to go by was the story his family passed down through generations. To most people, we are fictional characters. All they have to rely on are books and old wives' tales. Authors like Bram Stoker have not helped our case.

"Is one night enough for him to know what our lives are like? Does he understand how we can hold back? Can we give him another chance? I think we should.

"I believe he will become remorseful. We understand that there are times that we have to kill, thankfully only in a few circumstances. I believe that deep down William regrets killing the vampires. Now that he is one, he doesn't think vampires are evil, and he will live by our rules. Thank you."

Susan rose. "Your Honor, may I offer a rebuttal?"

"It's not normal procedure, but I'll allow it."

"Thank you, Your Honor.

"So, we didn't judge him until he became one of us. We treated him like we would treat any new vampire. He got the rules that we live by. And on the second night, William made his choice–to kill again. He enjoyed the killing. William would kill, whether as vampire or as human.

"We don't have the luxury of waiting for him to change. If we have the proper teacher when we learn to be a vampire, then we don't want to kill when we don't have to. We try to stop other vampires who go on killing sprees. There is nothing different here. William Chemberlin's behavior when killing the second victim shows he just likes to kill. We would eventually have come to the same conclusion. We are saving human lives by passing judgment now. Thank you."

"Thank you all," said the judge. "Jury, you are to find the defendant guilty or not guilty. Part of your job is determining whether he will be a good vampire–indeed, is he worthy to be a vampire? Now, to your duty."

"Solena," said Edmond, as he came toward me and John. "I think they will find him guilty."

"I don't know, Edmond. I know he is not worthy to be a vampire. I want him dead. But I will abide by the court's decision."

"That is what should be done. Solena, I'm glad I came back."

"I am too, Edmond. I have missed you. The children have missed you–and now they have their father back."

"Solena, am I not their father?"

"John, Edmond is their first vampire father. You are both very special to them. They love you both. But they spent their first 200 years with Edmond and me. He made my daughters, which are his daughters."

"John," said Edmond, "I am glad there was someone else to be their father. I have missed being their father. They are lucky–they have two. There is more love to go around."

"Edmond?"

"Yes, Solena."

"What are you going to do after the sentence is passed?"

"I figure I will stay around here. Josephine and Alexander have offered me a place to stay. Richard is thinking of going back home. He likes England. He will linger for a while to get to know all of us. ... Oh, looks like the jury is back."

"That didn't take long!" I said.

Everyone returned to the courtroom.

"I call this court back into session," Judge Shari declared.

The jury came in.

"Do you have a verdict?"

"We do, Your Honor."

"Will the defendant please rise? Jury, what say you?"

"We find the defendant guilty on all counts. We also find he is not worthy of being a vampire."

"Thank you. You are dismissed.

"William Chemberlin, you have been found guilty and I must pass sentence. You are going to die. You are going to be executed the same way you killed the two vampires. Brad, take him to his cell."

With help, Brad dragged Willy away.

Back in the cell Brad asked Willy, "Why didn't you tell me what you felt, so I would have known what questions to ask you? I agree with the jury, because I am a vampire. I am just sorry about how you are going to die. You should make peace with yourself. I regret that you can't say goodbye to your family, but they know you are not coming back. Somebody will come and get you. Do not fight them, or you will die anyway the next night."

"I won't fight them."

"Now, please make peace with what you believe to be your Maker. You didn't give the vampires you killed the chance. I am being merciful, and the court is too. They could have decided even closer to sunrise."

"I will make my peace, but I don't think it will help. Please leave me alone."

"Of course. By the way, don't try to stab yourself or kill yourself another way. Those ways won't kill you. And there is no wood in here."

Brad left.

"Well, you won, Susan. I'm glad you did."

"Thanks, Brad. I too am glad I won. The world will be better when he is gone. That will be three Chemberlins killed by vampires. But I don't think this Chemberlin will be going like the other two. He killed two people when he didn't have to. I think I should go talk to Solena Wilshire. I bet she is very happy."

"Yes, just like every vampire in New York!"

"Solena, we haven't met yet. I was the Prosecutor."

"Yes, you questioned me, but we haven't met otherwise. This is my husband John, and these are my three children, Annabelle, Josephine, and Arthur, and their spouses Doug, Alexander, and Jessica."

"Pleased to meet all of you."

Kathy and Edmond walked up.

"Oh, yes, this is Kathy, my granddaughter."

"You have a granddaughter?"

"Yes, she is Josephine and Alexander's daughter."

"Nice to meet you," said Kathy. "You were the Prosecutor?"

"Yes, I was. I'm glad the deed is done. I wish I could watch this in person."

"We all wish we could," said Edmond. "Susan, it's nice to talk to you again–and this time, not from the witness stand!"

"This is a much nicer way."

"Are you going home, or staying here a while?"

"I live in France. I will be flying back there."

"The sun will be rising in about an hour," John remarked. "We should be getting home. The rest of the vampires are leaving. Solena, are you ready to go?"

"Yes, I am, John."

"Susan, it was nice to meet you."

"Thanks, John."

They left.

Two vampires came to get Willy. He went with them calmly. They put him in a special room. It didn't look so different from the cell. But when the door was closed, the room changed.

Crosses appeared on every wall. Then the roof opened. Willy was stuck right where the sun would be. He couldn't look at the crosses–they burned his eyes. So he looked up in the sky, and prayed to his god. He begged for mercy.

About a quarter of an hour later the sun began to rise. He ran to one of the corners, but the crosses stopped him. He was trapped in every direction. Willy could feel his skin burning. He screamed. He could see the flames on his skin. When the sun was fully in the sky, his entire body burst into flame. Nothing was left.

Every vampire in New York could hear the screams. They knew they were finally safe. William Chemberlin was dead.

The lives of the vampires went back to normal.

Richard went back to England without Edmond. Edmond stayed to be with his other family.

Some mornings, when the sun is about to rise, I think about all the vampires William Chemberlin and his family killed. And how I could have died if it hadn't been for my friends and family. How lucky I am to have them!

I also think about William Chemberlin and how he wasted his life. We vampires don't want to waste our lives.

And every once in a while, when I think about William Chemberlin, a single tear falls from my eye.

Because I too–a vampire–have a heart.

EPILOGUE

The Willy Chemberlin trial and execution took place thirty years ago. Since then, vampires and humans have managed to live together without incident. There will undoubtedly be vampire hunters again. I wouldn't say we're on edge, but we're not lackadaisical either. We can mobilize on a moment's notice.

At a time when immigrants and refugees–indeed, whoever can be lumped into the category of "other"–are in jeopardy from white supremacists, vampires could be targeted by human supremacists. "Vampires are trying to destroy our human civilization!" "Vampires won't replace us!"

I hope it's clear from my story that these fears are groundless. I suppose we can't ever be fully assimilated–for instance, we're always absent from the half of activity that takes place in daylight– but we're not subversive, not out to "Make Vampirica Great Again." To put it simply: We want to mean something, not live wasted everlasting lives.

If you come to New York and are looking for "the best 'sex' you ever had," call By the Light of the Moon. We're still in business.

And while we don't really advertise, we can assure you that you are safe. In these times we are wearing masks whenever they are mandated, and we have all been vaccinated. ("Social distancing," of course, is not an option in our line of work.) These actions are totally unnecessary, but our safety depends on our blending in, not attracting attention.

You see, vampires are completely immune to all bacteria and viruses that have ever been, are now, and will evolve in the future. We can make you immortal. We cannot make you sick.

You're probably wondering: How has the Solena-Edmond-John triangle fared?

In order to minimize friction, I made a decision almost the moment Edmond reappeared.

At the beginning of this memoir I introduced myself as Solena Wilshire Chilstrom. This seemed appropriate, since it was as such that I was known for nearly a thousand years. But then: Was I henceforth to be called "Mrs. Edmond Chilstrom" or "Mrs. John Anderson"? The solution? Neither. Inspired by the feminist revolution, I'm simply what I was the day I was born: Ms. Solena Wilshire. You may have noticed that I was referred to this way throughout Willy's trial.

The name didn't forestall all problems. The triangle has had its moments of up and down–indeed, it's by turns equilateral, isosceles, scalene, obtuse, acute, and right–but so far, no explosions. And, after all, we have forever to figure it out ...